SEA *of* TREES

A Novella by
Robert James Russell

Winter Goose Publishing

Winter Goose Publishing
2701 Del Paso Road, 130-92
Sacramento, CA 95835

www.wintergoosepublishing.com
Contact Information: info@wintergoosepublishing.com

Sea of Trees

ISBN: 978-0-9851548-5-1

COPYRIGHT © 2012 by Robert James Russell

First Edition, May 2012

Cover Art by Winter Goose Publishing
Typeset by Victoriakumar Yallamelli
Published in the United States of America

For Patty

Hope

She touches the bark of a tree, traces it with her fingers like she's familiar with it, seen it before. I see her only barely through the endless green, slivers of her that pop into view for a moment. I stop and take a drink of water, hot and tired, but force a smile, pretending as if I'm enjoying this as much as she seems to be, just in case she's looking.

"There is something carved in it," she says, waving at me. "Come look."

I make my way up the narrow path to where Junko is, navigating the lava rock formations that jut out in severe patterns, dodging the ankle-shattering holes and fissures that dot most of the trail, and finally force my way through a few feet of thick brush. When I find her she's standing between two trees, looking beautiful, her hair pulled back into a tight ponytail, some sweat on her forehead and cheeks that she doesn't pay any attention to, pointing at the bark, smiling.

"Do you see?"

"What is it?"

"Someone must have put it here a long time ago."

I move in closer, put my hand on the small of her back. I feel her relax into my grip, and look at the symbols carved into the bark. "What does it say?"

"I'm not sure," she says furrowing her brow and leaning closer to the tree, tracing her fingers across the marks. "It is worn out. I wonder if it was someone who . . ."

She stops suddenly, looks back at me and then back into the woods surrounding us.

"It could've been some children or something. Teenagers, maybe," I say, trying to comfort her.

"Mmm," she says still not looking at me. I try to pull her close again, to feel her against me, but she resists, says, "I think we should keep going."

"Sure."

Junko puts on her backpack and starts back toward the path, her slim legs poking out of those khaki shorts I love so much, the bulky hiking boots she just had to buy looking rather clownish on her. I look at my watch: ten-thirty am. We walk in silence for the next thirty minutes, stopping only occasionally to drink water and search in our immediate vicinity for any sort of evidence that Izumi had been there. At one point I ask her what she hopes to find, but she doesn't look at me, meticulously checking a fallen tree trunk, determined like I've never seen her before.

Sometime later we emerge from a particularly covered area of the woods at a crossroads and see two brightly painted signs. We squint as we approach, the forest opening up here a bit, allowing us to see unfiltered daylight for the first time since we started the hike. The first sign, a map of the woods, tells you exactly where you are with a painted red arrow, and where each direction will take you, the length of the loops, and areas that are off limits to visitors. Junko and I study it, the sheer size of Aokigahara, and it makes me laugh.

She's looking at me for the first time in what seems like an eternity. "What is so funny?" she asks and I'm thrown off by this, by her beautiful eyes as if it's the first time I've seen them again.

"Nothing. It's just, this place is so big." I gesture to the expanse of trees surrounding us.

"That is why so many Japanese come here," she says quietly, with some disdain. "No one will find their bodies that way, or stop them before they go through with it."

I stop, move closer to her and spin her around so she's facing me. I touch her shoulders, close to her neck, and feel the sweat, her skin smooth, inviting. "I wasn't making fun of you."

"I know," she says. "I just really need to do this. To be here."

"And you really think we'll find something?"

She looks up at me, smiles, and presses her head against my chest. "I . . . am not sure."

"Well, we'll try our best, right?"

"Right," she says looking up at me. I study her face, the tiny mole on her left cheek, her lips, and lean in to kiss her. She acts surprised at first but gives in, kissing me hard, fast, until she finally peels herself away, wiping her lips clean. She steps back and smiles, looks embarrassed.

I point to a smaller sign tacked to a nearby tree written in nothing but Japanese characters. "What does this one say?"

Junko approaches and reads through it a few times, nodding her head, taking it all in, then: "It says, 'Your life is a precious gift from your parents. Think about them.'"

I stand back and look around the path. The forest is quiet, no animal noises, no insects buzzing, no gusts of wind caus-

ing trees to knock together and no children playing unsu-
pervised nearby or family picnics and happy memories being
made. Just nothing. The sky is gray, has been all morning,
and I set my pack down for a moment, stretching my back.
Junko sees me and does the same.

"Want me to carry your bag a bit?" I ask.

"What? No," she says, concerned.

"Are you sure? It looks heavy."

"You are already carrying your pack. I do not need you to
carry mine."

"Relax. I'm just trying to help."

She stops, composes herself. "Sorry. I am just anxious. Do
you understand?"

"Yeah, I do. What did you put in there, anyway? I thought
we were only packing some food and water."

"Just some of Izumi's things."

"Can I see?"

"Not now." She forces a smile.

"Sure. Fine."

"What time is it?"

"Eleven-fifteen."

"I would like to keep moving," she says picking her pack
up. I watch as she puts it on, then pulls her hair free from her
ponytail. She runs her hands through it a few times, and ties
it back tight, checking quick to make sure it's in place. She
sees me watching her and smiles, blushes a bit.

"Well, which way?" I look quick in both directions, seeing
nothing but the same: a worn path of dark earth disappearing in two directions, an army of trees straddling them on

both sides, and darkness under the canopies.

"This way," she says moving left. East.

"Are you sure?"

"It feels right," she says and starts moving, not waiting for me. I watch her for a moment before I start following, watch her disappear into the shadows of the woods again, watchful as she passes by every whorled and knotty tree, reading into the patterns of the bark as if they'd give us some clue to Izumi's last days, what path she chose in this labyrinth, the only sound in this entire place her feet as they march on, beating hard against the ground.

On her sixteenth birthday, Yui Sato had had enough, locked herself in the toilet, and attempted to kill herself by mixing detergent and bath salts—her mother's—a method she had researched on the internet. She sat on the cold tile floor as the mixture turned into a thick white gas and quickly filled the room, breathing in the pungent fumes for nearly five minutes before her father, Haruki, managed to force his way in and rushed to open the window. Haruki and the rest of the family— her mother, Mako, and younger brother, Koji—were in the den watching television and the moment she saw her father's eyes she wished she hadn't acted so quickly and waited until she was alone—it had been the rotten egg smell that had given her away.

Months later the incident was nearly forgotten, Haruki buried in his work, Mako withdrawn and tending almost exclusively to Koji during his impeding adolescence. Yui was forced to talk to a counselor about her actions, and out of those sessions she developed a desire to have a better future, being told that, among other things, she deserved one—that the light would most certainly present itself to her. So Yui came to renounce the selfish act, and as similar deaths were reported on the news, all successful in her method—a twelve-year-old girl in Nakano City, a forty-year-old man in Kita, among others—she laughed at what she had almost accomplished, the desperate acts of a young girl starving for attention.

But on her seventeenth birthday, something changed in Yui again—the dreams she had been cultivating in the previous year, all of the wishful thinking and daydreams, came up short, or not at all. So she became withdrawn again, skipped school, stopped seeing her friends entirely and, when at home, holed herself up in her room, on her computer. She became fascinated with the rising number of Japanese who commit suicide, trying hard to understand the phenomena among her people. This lead, naturally, to her thoughts settling on the more philosophical ramifications of death, concluding finally that this world had nothing left for her, and that the next—even one she would be propelled into by her own hands—would have to be better.

So Yui set about planning—this time down to every meticulous detail—the different ways in which she could kill herself without interference, deciding the further from home she could go the better for all it would be. She knew how she would do it—quick and to the point, but not where, and then, suddenly, it appeared to her: Aokigahara. She had heard stories all her life of those woods, of the folklore and how people went there to do the unthinkable, to die in peace amongst the trees, and when she saw a news report about the unprecedented number of bodies found there by the Suicide Patrols—dancing images of the lush landscape caked with lava rock and various leafy trees, a far cry from her life in Tokyo—she decided almost immediately to trade one endless abyss for another, preferring, she thought, the endless green to the endless neon.

A week later her plans were set: She would eat breakfast with her family, kiss Koji on his head, hug her parents, and leave for school—only this time, she would take the train to Shinjyuku Station, the Chuo Expressway bus to Kawaguchiko Station, and finally, ninety minutes later, a local bus to Aokigahara. When the day came, she was surprised at how she felt: no remorse, no fear. She enacted her pre-set motions like a skilled actress, all of them performed many times in her head leading up to it, no one suspicious that she would not be returning. She tucked a small note in her favorite book left on her bed, a simple letter telling her family that she loved them, because she did, and began her journey.

No one spoke to Yui that morning, not at the stations or the crowded trains nor the conductor of the buses she took. When she emerged from the final bus at the entrance to Aokigahara, a sparsely-occupied parking lot where day hikers would come—a trailhead—she felt relieved. And when she first felt the dark soil beneath her feet, a confidence washed over her. She passed few hikers, many of whom paid no attention to her, just a girl out for a hike, and trekked deeper into the silent woods, the woods with the towering trees blocking out the grey sky. After she had been hiking for two hours, significantly out of the way of watchful and concerned eyes, determined to find the perfect spot, emerging finally into a small clearing surrounded on all sides by dark trees with knotted bark that wisped up crooked toward the sky. She smiled: this was it.

Yui lay on the ground at the center of the small clearing and waited thirty minutes like that, still and silent, listening to the woods speak to her. She was desperately hungry, but it didn't matter anymore—nothing did. She tried to shush images of her family grieving, finding the note and trying to determine its meaning, and, unsuccessful, decided it was time, lest she ponder on such things longer and lose her nerve. She pulled from her pack a shaving razor—her father's—and removed the blade from it. She held it up, glinting in the bits of sun that filtered down from the canopy, and with no grand speech, no last words of any kind, ran it across both wrists lengthwise, slicing her arms *open, blood pouring onto her lap and staining the ground be-neath her dark. She smiled sweetly: there was no pain, just a warmth, and she lay back again, looking at the trees and leaves and sky, finding, for the first time in her life, her place in this world among them.*

Respect

There was a car in the parking lot of the main trailhead leading into the forest—an eggshell-colored Isuzu four-door
dimpled with rust and dents—that had been abandoned for
three months, we had been told by a sad-looking woman
before she drove off. The owner, whoever it was, had walked
into the woods and never come out, presumed dead. Like
the rest of them. Junko and I looked through the dirty win-
dows as if we were shopping, finding nothing of notice inside except a used chemistry textbook and a Tokyo Yakult
Swallows baseball hat.

I don't know why, but now, having been hiking for almost
three hours, I start thinking about it again, about what happened to the owner.

"Remember that car in the parking lot?" I ask.

Junko stops, still a few paces ahead of me, and wipes her
forehead clean. "Which car?"

"That white one. With the textbook on the front seat."

"Oh, yes."

"Why do you think he came here?"

"What makes you think it was a man?"

"Well, good point. Whoever it was, what do you think
their story is?"

"I do not know," she says. "And I do not think it is right
for us to decide."

"I don't want to decide, but it's quiet here, and I think it would help if we talked."

"It is not right to speak of the dead," she says stopping and looking back at me, scolding.

"But we don't know if they are dead."

I wait for a moment and take a drink of water. Junko walks over to me, smiles, and grabs the bottle, taking a drink herself. "Maybe he hanged himself."

"You think?"

"Many of the bodies they find here . . . they chose that method," she says handing the water back and looking back toward the path, away from me. "That is what I heard, anyway."

"I hope not. That's a horrible way to go."

"Let's get going," she says. "We still have much more to go."

"To be fair, we still have the whole forest, and we really don't know where to go. I mean, we're just prancing along here, hoping we'll find something, right?"

"As opposed to what?" she says staring at me, scowling. "Just going home? Giving up?"

"No, but the chances we'll find something on a trail like this, on one of the main trails, is . . . probably not very good. That's all I'm saying."

"There are some smaller trails up ahead, some that go closer to Saiko Lake. I would like to go in that direction. Izumi . . . she loved the water."

I look around again at the trees, at the path we're on, and force a smile. "As long as we're back to the car by sunset, we can go wherever we need to."

"Thank you, Bill," she says touching my hand. "It means so much that you would come with me."

"Of course," I say, not sure if I really mean it or not. "I'm going to go to the bathroom quick, before we go, okay?"

She nods and her smile fades. I head away from the path and up a small incline through a particularly thick group of trees, looking back every few steps to keep an eye on Junko, her eyes searching the woods, constantly looking for something. I navigate through the trees, the bark smooth to the touch as I pass by, when suddenly I see it: a pile of knick-knacks near a large, especially knotty tree, personal artifacts left behind, the first real glimpse of someone else having been here. I move closer, nervous, but I'm not sure why, and kneel, taking stock of what I see: a pink hairbrush with strands of long dark hair still twisted around the head, a pair of torn black leather gloves, a half-empty can of hairspray, a compact wedged open (the mirror inside cracked in half), letters written in Kanji, and a pair of large-framed glasses, lenses still intact. I kneel next to the pile and wonder why it got dumped here, of all places. If the owner got fed up trudging through the forest and decided this was the best place to get rid of all their earthly possessions.

"Hey," I shout back toward the path at Junko. "Come and look."

I can hear her approach on the thick layer of dried leaves and sticks along the ground and she lets out an audible gasp when she sees the items. I turn to look at her and she looks scared, nervous, and I hadn't thought that these could belong to Izumi. I stand and face her.

"What . . . is this?" she asks, still at a distance.

"I just found some stuff is all. I don't know . . . if it's hers."

She peeks around me, afraid to come any closer, and meets my gaze again. "Is there a stuffed bear?"

"Stuffed bear? No."

"I had given one to her when we were younger. She took it with her everywhere."

"Well, maybe these things aren't hers, then. Do you . . ." I stop, rub my head, and watch her for a moment. Then: "Do you want to check it out and see? Just to be sure?"

She nods and takes a few steps forward, testing the ground as if it may fall out from under her, and mentally sifts through everything, still standing. "What is that paper?"

"Looks like a letter. Do you want to see it?"

"Yes," she says folding her hands together, playing with them to distract herself.

I grab the papers, half a dozen or so, and clean the dirt off. I flip through them at first, but can't make anything out, and hand them over. I watch Junko's face as she begins reading, looking for a sign, anything, scanning the lines of text. After a minute of silence, I see her mouth curl up slightly: a smile.

"This is not her," she says excitedly. "This is someone called Mai."

"Well, that's good," I say. "What else do they say?"

She reads again, flipping through them. "She had committed adultery, and her husband had found out. He had kicked her out, and she came here, unsure of what to do."

I look back at the pile of items, then out to the woods, a puzzling kaleidoscope of browns and grays. I turn back to

Junko and she's folding the pages up neatly. "So she kills herself because she made a mistake? A bit drastic, isn't it?"

"You do not understand," she says handing the pages to me, stern, angry. "We are a very proud people. Very traditional in many ways. It is very hard for some to live with themselves after they have done something so horrible."

"Well, that's crazy."

"Maybe, but that is how it is," she says and takes a few steps back, looking at the trees again, running her hand up and down the bark of one nearby.

I look down at the papers and place them back with the other things. By the time I turn back, Junko is scurrying off toward a small hill that almost looks like a wave rising from the forest floor. "Where are you going?" I shout after her.

"Exploring!"

"Can you not just run off, please?" I say chasing after her. By the time I reach the hill she's just about at the top, climbing over pieces of rock and through interlocking trunks of trees, standing tall at the crest like a proud warrior. I follow, surprisingly out of breath, and drop my pack to the ground when I meet her, tired, wondering how, in all the excitement, in the heat, she's still wearing hers. Then I see she's not looking at me, not noticing me at all, but looking down in the small valley at a neon-yellow tent perched in a clearing. "What is that?"

"Someone camped here," she says soberly, staring straight ahead.

"Maybe they're still around here somewhere," I say, standing. "Maybe they're looking for someone too."

"Could be," she says.

We wait for a minute, the quiet of the woods creeping back on us, and unable to take it any longer, I shout: "Hello? Anyone there?" Junko hits me, tells me to be quiet, to not disturb. I don't listen and add: "We're coming down!"

"What are you doing?" she says as I put my pack back on.

"It would be nice to see another person, if someone is there."

"And if there is not?"

"Then nothing to worry about, right?" I say, smiling, descending the hill. She quickly follows and we navigate the slope until we get to the bottom, Junko glued to me, her hands around my arm. "Hello?" I call out again.

"Empty," she says quietly.

"I guess so."

We stop about ten feet from the tent and study the surroundings, noticing yellow tape tied to nearby trees like police tape at a crime scene. I walk over to a loose strand and pick it up, showing it to Junko. "What is this place?"

"I do not know," she says. "Maybe . . . we should go."

"Let's at least check out what's inside the tent. Maybe it belonged to the woman from the letters?" I drop the yellow tape and move to the entrance of the tent, which is zipped completely up. I look back at Junko, who looks truly frightened for the first time since we've been here, and I smile. "I promise it'll be fine."

The zipper's stubborn but I manage to slide it open, finding only a sleeping bag that smells like mildew, a few fashion-style magazines, and empty water bottles.

"What is it?" she says from behind me, safely away.

"Nothing, just some water bottles and a sleeping bag."

"No body?"

"Nope. It's clean," I say turning around to face her. "I wonder if—" I stop, frozen, seeing the shape of a wilted man behind Junko, near the tree line, watching us, leering at us, his hair grayed in sections, wearing a red tracksuit, a walking stick in hand, and once it registers, really sinks in, I lurch almost a foot backward into the tent itself. "Oh, shit!" I manage to get out.

Junko looks behind her and likewise sees the man, jumping a bit, moving back toward me in the tent. I get up as quickly as I can and stand in front of her, protecting her, the old man standing perfectly still, staring right at us as if we don't belong. Then, finally, after this stand-off of no talking, we see him lick his lips and take a step forward, toward us.

"You should not touch those things," he says in English, his Japanese accent surprisingly light. "If a body had been in there, it can produce germs and disease. Anything it touches. You would not want such things on your skin."

"Is this . . . are you camping here?" I manage to get out.

"No," he says stepping forward again. "I am here to pay my respects."

"Oh," I say brushing myself off. "Sorry to hear."

"And you two as well?"

I look to Junko who looks at the old man, nervous, not like the Junko I know, the hard-party bar girl taking shots and dancing, not afraid to talk to anyone, someone else entirely here, in her skin. I touch her shoulder and she steps back, surprised, and relaxes when she realizes it's just me. "The same," I say back.

"Well, we should not be here. The Suicide Patrols, they mark off these areas, where people have left their things behind." He points with his walking stick, a long, crooked piece of wood that's no more than a branch, really. "Let's go back to the trail, where it is safe."

"Fine by me," I say, smiling at Junko, nudging her. We watch as the old man turns away from us, toward the woods, back toward the path, and follow as he leads us away from the tent. I try to hold Junko's hand and she lets me for a moment, then stops, dropping mine. "What's wrong?"

"Nothing," she says.

"I know this is all pretty heavy, being here and all, but are you sure you're okay?"

"Fine," she says looking back at the tent before it disappears, the woods enveloping us again. "Perfectly fine."

On an October night Ken Suzuki was approached about work by a man named Ryohei Mitsuru—a Yakuza enforcer better known as Toro. Ken had run into Toro a few times before within the small circle of friends he had, a man he had never spoken a word to, but feared, as they all did, due to his association with the "chivalrous" organization. So when Ken received a call from Toro requesting a meet, he did what anyone in the know would do: obliged.

"It is in the forest," he said pulling him into a small hostess club. "Aokigahara."

Ken smiled, took a drink of the whiskey the beautiful hostess brought for them. "Oh, that forest."

"You do not want the job? I was told that you have been out of work for quite some time. I am sure your family would be proud of you to earn a wage."

"Yes, but . . . Aokigahara is—"

"Only a forest. Besides, for a single day you will make more than you have had all year."

"And if I say no?"

"It is a job offer, not a command. But—" He finished his whiskey. "—it is never bad to have me owe you a favor."

Ken took a drink. "Yes, I suppose not."

"Do you still see Jun?"

"Jun?"

"Do not be so afraid," Toro said. "We have mutual friends. And I know Jun . . . a little, anyway. I had heard you and she were together."

"Oh, well, not any longer, no."

"What happened?" Toro said watching him intensely, wait-

ing for an answer.

"We drifted apart is all," Ken said looking at the floor, then at the beautiful hostesses, never at Toro's eyes. "It happens."

"Yes it does. Well, perhaps it is for the best. Besides, there are many other Juns in Japan. Maybe she was not the right Jun."

Ken laughed nervously, finished his drink, and for the first time noticed tattoos peeking out from under Toro's jacket cuffs. "So, when do you need me?"

"Tomorrow."

"And what is it I would be doing?"

Toro stood, removed a folded piece of paper from his pocket and handed it to Ken as he made his way for the door. "Your partner will fill you in tomorrow."

"Partner?"

The next morning Ken found himself dressed in a green ski jacket borrowed from his father—although he did not tell his purpose, just that he had found work—and met a man named Toyama at Shinjuku Station who likewise had been drafted by Toro. The two men exchanged pleasantries and boarded a train for Otsuki, an hour's ride, and it wasn't until the final leg—via bus—that Toyama informed Ken about what it was they would be doing in Aokigahara.

"Jukai has its share of visitors, as I am sure you are aware, many who never return. The Suicide Patrols and the police, they only find a handful of the bodies every year. The woods are . . . twisted and confusing. Very easy to lose your way in there. So Toro and others like him, they draft people like us, maybe out of work, or homeless, to go in and loot the bodies, take anything of *value."*

"Rob them?"

"Well, they cannot very well use their belongings now, can they?"

"I suppose not, no."

"So we will go in and relieve them of their things, bring them back to Toro."

"And we will be paid for this?"

"Yes, and—" Toyama looked around, made sure no one was listening. "—no one will know if we keep some for ourselves."

"Are you sure?"

"The wage Toro will pay is good, but not great. There is no map of these bodies, so he will not have to know what we did and did not pass by. That is . . . if I can trust you."

Ken thought hard. "I do not see why not."

"Yes. Exactly. Some of these people have some nice things on them."

"Maybe I will find a watch . . . for my father?" Ken said aloud, watching out the window.

Toyama studied him. "Yes. Anything is possible in Aokiga-hara."

The two made their way into the forest in the early afternoon along a pre-determined route that had been assigned to them by Toro. There were no cars in the visiting parking lot they passed through, no discernible hikers they could see, and it was some time before either man spoke.

"It is so quiet here," Ken said finally.

"That is the first thing you all say," Toyama said.

"There are others?"

"I have been here a dozen times now, I believe. Give or take. Every time I find it more beautiful than the last."

"I find it very unsettling," Ken said as they passed an especially warped and knotted tree trunk that looked like a face peeling away from the wood.

"The first visit will do that. But now when I come, I find it very peaceful. Very . . . romantic."

They continued on, finally discovering a body—a young man, a teenager. Ken watched as Toyama put on plastic surgeon gloves— "For the germs," he said—and checked the boy's pockets, flipping him over onto his back and revealing his sunken face, the flesh tight and in the thralls of decay. Ken was surprised at how easy it was to look at him, that the fear he assumed would wash over him—since he had never seen a dead body before—never came. Even when his turn came when they happened on a middle-aged woman, mostly skeleton now with mats of hair and skin stuck to a piece of the coat she still wore, Ken was at ease checking her for jewelry, money, anything of value they could pocket or bring back to Toro.

As they continued deeper into the woods, Toyoma taught Ken the most ideal places to look for bodies, where and when the Suicide Patrols came (as well as parts of the forest they refused to venture), and how to interpret the many signs along the trails so as not to get lost, "Easy to do," he said. Ken had looted half a dozen bodies by dinner time, and as they ate the meals they had packed, hunkered down not far from the trail, they shared with one another the most interesting items they had picked up.

"Not as good today," Toyoma said. "Someone else has been through recently, I think."

"I found some nice things," Ken replied as he ate.

"Let me see."

Ken emptied his pockets on the ground: a few pieces of jewelry, personal items belonging to a girl (make-up, a comb, etcetera), a few coins. "What do you think?"

"Worthless," Toyoma said picking through the things. "Except the jewelry. I will hold on to that."

He picked up the ring and a necklace, admired them, and stuffed them in his coat. "I think there is a camp up the hill behind us. Would you mind taking a look while I finish eating?"

"Shouldn't we be leaving soon?" Ken looked up at the sky— what sky he could see, anyway—noticing traces of night already on the horizon. "It is starting to get dark."

"Yes, soon. But we should check this last spot."

"Sure."

Ken made his way up the small hill as Toyoma watched him. By the time he had gone up and over, he found a body—another woman, but no camp—and proceeded to check it as he had been taught. He was busy in his work, finding a scrap of paper with directions written on it, more coins, and so did not hear Toyoma approach from behind, or take out from inside his large jacket a long, thin knife. In fact, it wasn't until he heard the final footstep of Toyoma approaching that he knew he was there at all, turning as the knife entered his side, between the ribs. Ken fell back to the ground, but not before Toyoma stabbed him twice more, near the first wound, both times puncturing so deep the pain was delayed and not noticeable until he took a step back to survey the damage.

He watched Ken writhe near the body of the woman, unable to speak, hands clutching the wounds as if it might help.

Toyoma looked at the knife, then back to Ken, and tossed it on the ground. "Toro says this is for Jun," he said.

"J-Jun? I do not understand." Ken said, forcing the words out.

"Jun Inoue is Toro's cousin. He knows you got her pregnant, made her get an abortion. Then you left her to be alone. Called her a slut."

"No, you do not understand—"

"It does not matter," Toyoma said. "This is the message I was to deliver. That you disgraced her, and now she is not the same, because of you. Toro wished for you to feel half of what she does."

"But—"

Toyoma kneeled. "To be honest, I think you are a good guy, from what I know, so I am sorry it has to be this way. But this was my job. I hope you understand."

Ken reached out, tried to grab a hold of Toyoma, but he stood, distanced himself. "You cannot . . . leave me . . ."

"I really thought you knew who Toro was," Toyoma replied, walking back toward the path. "How could you not? Or, maybe you did not want to see . . ."

Toyoma disappeared over the hill and it took another few minutes before Ken processed that he was truly alone, dying slowly—painfully—next to a woman who had reached a similar fate of her own doing. As he lay there along the ground, near her, he looked up at the trees and thought of Jun and of what he had done—perhaps it was the death that had a hold on him now, but he felt remorse for his actions for the first time. Ken truly had loved her, but acted like a child, so perhaps this was for the best.

He then thought of the hours to come, the life slowly slipping away, and even though no one would be around to see, he decided he would do the right thing—as well as the quick thing, to save himself from a long and agonizing end—to account for his sins against Jun. He managed to pull himself up and find the knife Toyoma had discarded, the blade soaked in his blood. He looked back to the woman behind him, imagining for a moment that she was Jun, that they were still together, and without thinking about it jammed the blade into his neck, going against every natural reaction to remove it, slicing deep and long in order to do the job right.

The last thing Ken saw was a torrent of red wash down his neck and hands, covering his lap, then his eyes glazed over as he faced the trees—the great trees of the forest—calling to him, welcoming him home, and, more than anything, forgiving him for what he had done.

Memory

"I am Seicho," the old man says once we're back on the main path. "You are American?"

"I am," I say. "My name is Bill."

"Nice to meet you," he says.

"Your English is very good."

"Ah, thank you. I taught in America for . . . twenty years. University of North Carolina."

"Oh, I'm from the Midwest. From Michigan."

"Mmm," he says nodding his head. "Great Lakes."

"Right," I say standing there, thinking, then: "What did you teach?"

"Philosophy," he says starting up the path again. "Retired many years ago. Moved back to take care of my parents."

I smile, look back to Junko who's looking anywhere but at me or Seicho, and we start following him. "This is my girlfriend, Junko," I say. "She's, uh, Japanese as well."

"I see that," Seicho says turning toward me, smiling. Then, nodding to Junko adds: "*Ha ji me ma hi te.*"

Junko nods back, says, "*Hai.*"

I smile at her and she meets my gaze for a moment then looks to the ground, seeming more concerned with where her feet are going as we start moving again. I look back to Seicho and he's stopped up ahead now, waiting for us, still smiling, his thin frame almost disappearing against the backdrop of the trees. As we approach his position I study him:

hair thick and gray, scruff hanging on his chin and jaw, eyes tired, deep wrinkles at the corners and along his mouth.

"So," I start, look around then back to him, "You lost someone here?"

"Yes. My son, Junji. Almost ten years ago."

"I'm sorry," I say, looking at Junko, trying to get her to respond in any small way, noticing her hands gripping the straps of her backpack tight.

"I come every month or so," he says. "I hike, pray, try to keep young people like yourselves from getting lost in the woods. It is very easy to do."

"Yeah, it's a maze in here."

"Mmm," he says, looking to the sky then back to us. "We should keep moving. We are almost there."

"Almost where?"

"The *hokura*," he says and starts up the path again. I look at Junko, unsure of what he means.

"It is a shrine," she says. "A small roadside shrine. Shinto."

"Oh."

We follow the path which narrows some then slopes up a small incline and back down, and see tucked between two large bushes at the side a small wooden shrine built up on a stack of large gray rocks, red paint faded from age and weather, Kanji characters painted in yellow along the side facing us.

"This is where you pray?" I ask.

"Yes, where I pray for my son."

We stand still for a moment before he gets to his knees and brushes some leaves off of the shrine, cleaning it, a small smile forming as if this small act brings him great joy.

"Back at the tent you mentioned something about a suicide team?"

"Suicide Patrol, yes," he says standing. "Part of the Japan Self-Defense Forces. Our national military. They come to the woods to look for bodies and people camping out who have not yet attempted to take their lives."

"And you're part of this Patrol?"

"Mmm. It is also made up of many volunteers. Last year we only found sixty bodies. I stopped five young men myself. I found them camping in the woods, talked them out of it and sent them back home. When I saw you two in the woods, at first I thought you had come here, like the others."

"No. Junko, she lost someone." I look back and Junko is glaring at me, not amused by my revelation to this man. This stranger.

"Excuse me," she says pulling out her MP3 player from her pocket.

She brushes past us, up the path but not too far away. She puts the headphones in and stares at the trees along the path, looking through them to the dark forest.

"I'm sorry," I say to Seicho. "This is all very emotional. Her sister . . . she came here a year ago."

"I am sorry," he says looking at Junko, studying her. "Were they close?"

"Very, I think. We . . . we met at university, six months ago. She asked me to come with her, to try to find some evidence of her, that Izumi had been here. Anything."

"For peace of mind."

"Yes, exactly. But truthfully," I say leaning in, "I told her not to get her hopes up. This place is massive."

"I think many feel as she does. They hope to come here, find a piece of clothing. A trinket. Something to make sense. But they rarely do."

"I can imagine."

"When I had heard about my son, I came here for a week. I was obsessed. But I found nothing, except a few other bodies, not his. And I built this *hokura* as something to represent him here. Something physical I could come and talk to."

I look at Junko, how beautiful she is, then to Seicho, who is looking back at the shrine. "To be honest, she's been acting odd since we got here. I think she hadn't expected it to be so difficult."

Seicho looks up at me, then into the trees overhead. "These woods, they are powerful. For centuries they were believed to be the home of *yurei*." He stops, looks at me, adds: "Ghosts."

"Oh."

"Even a generation ago some would bring the elderly to these woods, those they could not care for . . . and they would leave them to die." He steps forward, past the shrine, rubbing his jaw. "Japan has a dark past like that. Remove the parts of society that do not work. Things most Westerners do not know."

"That's awful," I say.

"Mmm." He walks over to the tree line behind the shrine and places his hand on a bare tree trunk, rubbing it gently. "There are dark memories here, of this place. And most Japanese are taught this as children. I think it should be hard here for her, or then you would have more to worry about."

"Good point," I say.

"Are you camping here tonight?"

"We just drove in for the day."

"That is good. Staying here for too long can be bad for your health, ghosts or not. Too much death has seen these woods, and it makes your mind think too much about such things."

"Well, don't worry about that. We brought just enough stuff for the day."

Seicho looks at me and smiles, then back down to Junko again. "It is an epidemic in this country, suicide. My son, Junji, we had a fight. Many bad fights. I did not agree with his lifestyle, with his choices. After the last fight he left, and I received a letter in the mail a week later telling me where he had gone and what he had done. It is hard not to blame yourself, even though it is their own actions. I think, for her, maybe she feels like she could have stopped her if she was here. If she was by her side."

"She doesn't talk to her family much anymore, because of everything. They all blame each other, think everyone else is at fault."

"These people, they are determined, for the most part. If they want to end their lives, they will. There is nothing anyone can do. The ones we save, they are the ones who are not sure yet. They are just thinking about it. The other ones, my son, her sister, there is nothing anyone can do, I think."

I nod, not saying anything, then check my watch and see it's already past two. "I actually think we need to get going.

She wants to try to get to the lake today, and we still have to make it back."

"Saiko?"

"I think so, yes."

"It is quite far still, goes off this main path here."

"Yeah, we saw the sign when we first came in. I told her we could go only quickly, look around, then head back."

"Here," he says taking off his backpack and rummaging inside for a moment, producing a stack of half-foot yellow ribbons. "Take these. The Suicide Patrol uses these to mark the trees near bodies, or camps. They are also useful if you find yourself going off the path into the woods. So you can find your way back."

"Thanks," I say grabbing them and looking them over. "So, if I see these in the woods . . . ?"

"It is possible that is where someone has died, yes."

I smile, nervous for the first time being here, putting them in my own bag. "Thanks for everything. For talking to me. It's a bit lonely out here. Even with the two of us."

Seicho extends his hand, smiling at first, then turning grave, serious, looking deep into my eyes. "Please be careful. There are many bodies still in these woods. Many that the volunteers will never be able to find. Bodies lost to all but the *yurei*. And if you find one, it can be very shocking. Very traumatizing for you both."

"Yeah, I'm hoping to avoid that, if we can."

"Mmm. Many come here hoping to find what you are, but leave changed. Aokigahara is a dark place, even in the daylight. Make sure you are back to your car by sunset."

"I will."

I start on my way, looking back at the tiny man in the red tracksuit kneeling again at the shrine, caring for it. When I reach Junko she's sitting on a tree stump next to the path, pulling her headphones out as I help her up.

"You really should have talked with him a little bit," I say.

She looks down the path at him, then back to me. "I did not come here to make friends," she says. "I came here to find Izumi."

"I know, but he was only trying to be nice. He even gave me some ribbons to tie on the trees, in case we go off the path."

"Oh," she says looking back at him. "Well, I doubt we will need them."

"Good to have anyway," I say, stroking her arm. She looks up at me, into my eyes. "Seicho told me that some people think there are ghosts here, in the woods. Have you heard that?"

"Many people say many things," she says pulling away from me. "It does not mean they are true."

"I know that. But you have to admit this place is creepy. What if we would've found someone in the tent, you know?"

"Then we will be careful the rest of the time, yes?"

"Yes. Very careful."

She steps away from me and stretches her back, her backpack weighing her down, but she doesn't remove it, so I reach out to try to help her, offering to hold it a while. When she sees me she freaks out, pushes my hand away. "What are you doing?" she asks, stepping back.

"It looks heavy. I just wanted to help."

"Well," she says stepping close to me again, "thank you but I am fine."

"Look, I'm here to help. I don't appreciate being treated like that."

"I just have personal things in here. Izumi's things that I thought I could place in the woods, if we find something. I feel . . . very protective."

"I get it, just . . . I'm on your side here, okay?"

"I know," she says, wrapping her arms around me again. "Izumi would have liked you."

"I'm sure I would've liked her too," I say kissing the top of her head. "C'mon, let's keep going. It's getting late and we still have quite a bit more to go."

Junko pulls away from me, still smiling, and I can't tell if it's forced or not. We start up the path and after a few steps I look back at Seicho, see him standing now and facing us, no expression on his face, studying us like he knows how it's all going to end.

In hindsight, Makoto should have seen it coming—he hadn't had anything to drink at the birthday party, his daughter Misaki's eighth—but the phone, his weakness, would not stop ringing, and every call seemed to be more important than the last, distracting him from the road and from getting them home safely during rush hour. And it was with the fourth call he received, from his boss, dodging a traffic light while checking his e-mail, when they were struck, hard, by a truck. By the time paramedics had arrived, Misaki was already unconscious, and Makoto, distraught and bleeding, desperately tried to get in touch with his wife, Noriko, who had stayed behind with friends.

It was later, at the hospital, after the doctors explained to Makoto and Noriko that Misaki had slipped into a coma, that Noriko slapped her husband and blamed him—that he could have prevented it if he had only been paying attention. He did not argue with her.

Weeks turned to months while Misaki lay there, neither getting worse or better. Makoto was there as often as he could be— he and Noriko, at first, would go together, but as the realization set in that their daughter, their little girl, might never wake up, their relationship began to crumble, impossible to repair, so eventually they took shifts at the hospital—Noriko during the mornings and afternoons, Makoto in the evenings, so they would not see one another. This continued for another seven months when, unexpectedly, the little girl opened her eyes among great rejoicing. Makoto was called at work, and when he arrived he was met by the doctor and Noriko—the first time he had seen her in weeks—her eyes swollen and red from crying.

"What is it?" Makoto pleaded. "I thought you said she was

awake? Can I see her?"

"Unfortunately," the doctor replied, "your daughter seems to have suffered brain damage from the accident. She will never truly be the same as she was before."

And she wasn't. Misaki—once bright and outgoing and full of energy—was now reduced to a catatonic state, hardly able to perform her own bodily functions, let alone communicate in any way. In fact, other than her eyes, which seemed to drink in all around her, there was no true visible sense she was there with them at all. Any chance of reuniting their family was now lost and Noriko, only a few days later, served Makoto with divorce papers, telling him that every time she looked at their poor daughter, she could only think of what he had done, and any love that used to exist between them had been replaced with a unyielding disgust. In fact, the last words Noriko spoke to him were: "We would all be better off with you dead, Makoto."

Time passed, and Misaki, under constant supervision, went to live with Noriko and her parents—Makoto was told explicitly that he was never allowed to visit them there. Everyone, it seemed, blamed him for what had happened to their sweet girl. And why shouldn't they, he thought, and his heart broke daily as the events, no matter how hard he tried, replayed in his mind. Noriko finally agreed to let Makoto see them in a park, in public, for a short period of time, and the entire length of the visit was spent with him crying and pleading for more opportunities to see their daughter. But Noriko, who now had sole guardianship of Misaki, would not allow such a thing, as she did not trust her ex-husband, and told him to enjoy the time he had with her while he had it.

After they parted ways, Makoto thought of what Noriko had told him, that they—everyone—would be better off without him, and realizing he alone was responsible for what had happened to Misaki, that his negligence was to blame and that he had failed as a parent on nearly every possible level, that Noriko was right. He would do the right thing and end his life and that maybe, perhaps, in his death, they all might be able to move on.

So Makoto found a place of quiet where he could be alone with his sins—Aokigahara—and took with him only a single photograph of the family in happier times, at the birthday party before the accident. The entire drive to the forest he cried, thinking of the hollow way his daughter looked at him in the park, more than likely, like everyone else, blaming him for her condition, reminding him he was indeed doing the right thing. At the parking lot he left the keys in the ignition and a letter on the driver's seat he had written to Misaki, a letter he hoped Noriko would read to her one day, apologizing for everything he had done, and deep in he began looking for the spot, the perfect spot, thinking of Misaki's face the entire time, her blank stare, what would have been if only he had been more careful. Makoto finally settled on a large cropping of rocks and, climbing carefully to the top—about eight feet or so, stacked on top of one another like crates—he looked down to see more of the jagged lava rock on the forest floor greeting him. He then pulled out the picture and kissed it, looked up to the tree tops and to the peaks of grey sky showing between the branches, and without thinking dove head first, hoping only that maybe, in another life, they might all forgive him for what he had done.

Beauty

"Izumi was a beautiful girl," Junko tells me while we're eating granola bars. "All of the boys wanted to date her in high school."

"I'm sure you were just as beautiful," I say between bites, smiling at her.

"No, she was more beautiful," she says, angry, looking at the ground and chewing slowly. "Do not tell me about my own sister, Bill. Especially when you did not know her."

I sit back and swallow, looking down at the dark rock we're sitting on next to the path. A slight breeze hits the tops of the trees. "I just meant," I say, slowly, "that I think you're beautiful too. I wasn't trying to tell you about her, okay?"

She looks up at me and finishes chewing, her expression blank. "There was a boy, Daiki. He was a year older, in Izumi's grade. He had asked her out for months, but she always said no. She said no to most boys."

"Why is that?" I ask, watching as Junko smiles a bit, kicking the dirt with her feet.

"It was her way. A game," she says. "She often said she did not want what other girls her age wanted. She . . . always thought of herself as a woman, even when we were just girls. So these boys, they were not what she wanted."

"Fair enough."

"Then one day Daiki asked me out. I was flattered. He was very handsome. Too handsome for me. My mother even said so. Told me to be lucky any boy would talk to me."

"That's awful."

"And I knew he had only asked me so he could be close to Izumi," she says, not acknowledging me. "But I was okay with it. Because, for a moment, I felt beautiful. Like her."

"What happened with him?"

She looks at me and smiles. "Izumi found out what he was doing, that he was using me. She took very private photographs of him, told him she would spread them around school if he ever came around again." She starts laughing. "She was very protective of me."

"She sounds like a good sister."

"She was," she says looking back to the ground again, thoughtful. Happy. Then: "Do you know where we are?"

I look at my watch: four-fifteen. "Well, we've been walking about an hour since we saw the last sign."

"How long until we take the trail to the lake?"

"I'm not sure. Maybe another thirty minutes?"

She sighs, loudly, finishes her granola bar and tucks the wrapper in her backpack. "This is taking much longer than I thought it would."

"Well, you can't just expect to walk in here and stumble on some sort of clue or something, right? I mean, you don't know anything that happened to her."

Junko goes quiet again, staring at the ground then back at me, angry. "I did not know what to expect. You know this."

"Exactly, so you shouldn't get your hopes up. And, to be fair, I don't like the idea of being out here any later than we need to."

"I will stay out here as long as I please," she says standing. "You can go back any time you want."

"I'm not leaving you out here alone. And I didn't say we had to leave now, but you have to be reasonable. There are dead bodies everywhere, and we have no idea where we're going or what we're looking for."

"I know perfectly well."

"Then just agree that we'll look a little bit longer then head back. Okay?"

"Not before we get to the lake."

"If we don't make it there soon, then we should forget the lake."

"No," she says, tears in her eyes. "The lake . . . we have to go there. I think . . . that is where she would have gone."

"I get it, but are we going to stay out here at the risk of getting ourselves lost?"

"There are people in the woods all the time, searching and looking. We would not be lost for long."

I'm angry now, annoyed, so I stand and pace, hands flailing. "Everything we've heard about this place, all the ghosts, all the stories . . . do you really want to end up like Izumi? Come here and never leave?"

I stop, breathing heavy, and realize what I said. I look over at Junko who's watching me, terrified and hurt.

"How could you say that?" she asks.

"I'm . . . sorry," I say, but she turns away from me and darts toward the woods, crying hard. "Hey, where are you going?" I wait for a response, hoping she'll turn around, but she doesn't. I wait a moment longer, but still there's nothing, so I shout after her: "I'm not going in after you. You have to come back eventually."

I jam the rest of my granola bar in my mouth and chomp loudly, sloppily. Minutes go by and all I can think about is leaving, waiting for Junko to come back, dragging her to the car and pretending like this never happened. Finishing this fucking crusade of hers. And then suddenly, amongst the silence, I hear it: a scream. Junko's scream. I leave my pack and dart into the trees, squeezing through narrow trunks and branches, feeling something scratch my neck as I move. I step over jutted pieces of the black lava rock, shouting her name, telling her I'm on my way and following her cries up a series of small hills and back down again until I find her in a small clearing surrounded by bigger rocks, kneeling in the dried leaves and groundcover, her pale skin glowing amongst the gray-brown backdrop, her hands covering her face.

"Are you alright?" I ask, panting as I approach down a narrow path in the rock. She remains in place, kneeling and crying hard. "What is it? Are you okay?"

She peels her hands away from her face, cheeks flushed and her eyes red. "There," she whispers, pointing in front of her.

I look and see one of the larger faces of rock, about ten feet tall with trees growing on top, tan-colored roots cascading down like fingers. And there, hanging flat against it, a body suspended from a rope slung over one of the trees atop, a noose tied tight around his neck. "Holy shit . . ." I say, stepping back, leaning against a nearby tree for support.

"I . . . came down here and saw . . . it," she says. "I . . . oh,

God . . ."

"It's okay." I help her up and hug her, turning her away from the body: male, early thirties, cheeks and eyes sunken like it's been here a while. He's wearing a blue parka and jeans and there's a large backpack at his feet, which are hovering only a foot or so above the ground.

"How . . . do you do that to yourself?" she asks still holding on to me, peeking up from my chest as I begin to lead us back the way I came.

"He probably jumped from the top of the rock. Broke his neck or something," I say.

"It is horrible."

"I know." We start navigating the woods back toward the path, making sure not to look back, only at the trees ahead of us. "I'm sorry about before, at the trail. I know we're both acting a bit weird here, but I just . . . I care for you. I don't want to see you get hurt."

"But I need you to understand that I cannot leave here without finding something of hers. Anything."

"Well, we'll do what we can," I say, kissing the top of her head.

"Thank you. That is all I want."

We walk a bit longer, Junko tucked under my arms, so small next to me. I look back every so often, watching as the trees grow thicker, hiding that place of death from us. The image of the man in blue burns in my mind and I wonder how it's possible to have so much beauty surrounded by so much death.

Haruka had wanted to die in Paris during fashion week, but it was not to be. With a busier schedule than usual, as well as a speaking engagement regarding Asian women in the fashion industry, she had no time to herself to accomplish the feat. So, as it had for many years, the desire to end her life faded for the time being as she walked the catwalk in high-end wear, attended parties and galas studded with film and television celebrities, was treated as if she, simply a girl from Japan, mattered in the grand scheme of things—and she bought into it, as she always did.

Tall and glamorous, it wasn't hard for Haruka to find things to occupy her time, sinful cordials of various sorts—drugs, men and women. But these high times were matched with low lows, periods of great unease where the burden of being the new "it" girl weighed heavily on her, and that one day her looks would fade—and everything that she had based her young existence on would be gone along with them. During these times she retreated to her apartment in Tokyo, alone, reading and writing poetry, posting on her blog and looking, desperately, for a connection, for someone to tell her that there was something noble about what she did. These times of solitude never lasted long, though: her popularity kept her phone ringing with jobs, e-mails crashing in by the hundreds, everyone who wanted a piece of her while she was still very much "it," and this pressure, this constant need she would feel to make everyone happy, to be very much the life of the party, ate away at her. She was a ghost, she decided: seen but not heard.

Haruka's most recent self-exile—back in Tokyo for three months before a six-week North American excursion filled with higher-profile jobs than she had previously been offered—seemed exceptionally discouraging to her: the busier she became, the more overworked she was, the more disenchanted she found herself. She wrote feverishly, lines of poetry, vague musings on the meaning of existence and what the point of it all was, declining lunch dates with friends and dinner dates with would-be suitors. She even contemplated that she more than likely suffered from some sort of severe depression, but it had gone unnoticed, forever, perhaps because no one wanted to look further than her splendid features, that no one wanted to believe someone like her, a true beauty, could be so flawed.

During this time, between regular Ambien-induced naps—the only way she was able to truly shut out the world—Haruka, in an attempt to make sense of her existence, of the very state of her constant unease, tried piecing together a timeline of when she began feeling like everything was so pointless, trying to pinpoint how and why it would have started. And during her subconscious digging she unceremoniously realized it had always been there like a pit inside her—that she could remember ever not feeling this way. This realization was a comfort to her, of all things, knowing this was part of her, that, perhaps, she had been broken since birth, and like that, a wave washing over her, the desire to end it all returned, but with less malice than before. Haruka, for the first time, saw this inevitable ending as her destiny—what she had been born to do. Others would work and have families, do things that inspire, but she, the current envy of the fashion world, the girl everyone wanted a piece of, would shine bright and then, suddenly, be gone, making the world a better place without her in it—and for the first time in a long while, it all made sense.

So Haruka wrote one last cryptic entry on her blog entitled "Hello, Forever", gathered the rest of her Ambien and some Zopiclone she had been given by a friend in Berlin, packed a light bag and pinpointed to the hailed taxi driver that Aokigahara was her destination. The drive was expensive—not that it mattered—but shorter than she had thought it would be. She told the driver when he dropped her that she was meeting a friend, so as not to raise suspicion, and he happily took her tip and zoomed off back toward civilization. In the forest she took the first dose of pills, admiring the trees, reaching out to touch the knotty bark and twisted limbs that fell near the path, and marveled at the quiet of the place, that even the birds seemed to stay away from this place of death—a solitude she had never felt before.

She moved deeper into the woods, studying everything from the dark rock formations and the path at her feet to the signs pleading for those thinking of ending their life to rethink and turn back. She swallowed pills at first by the pair, then in groups of four and finally, an hour and a half into her trek, finding it harder to keep going, her limbs reacting sluggishly to her thoughts, the pills taking effect, she finished the last of them—eighteen in total, she thought, or perhaps nineteen. She could feel the sleep take hold of her, more forceful now, the warmth of her very last moments on earth, and she found a spot up a small hill a ways form the main path, a place of solitude for her, and lay down, admiring the scene around her, wondering how long until they had forgotten her—not long, she figured—and how better they would all be after she was gone. And, for the first time in as long as she could remember, as her eyes shut and the world went black around her, Haruka smiled.

Promise

The large wooden sign staked along the path is half-gone, torn almost in two, some graffiti written on the in-tact part which Junko tells me says "There is no God. There is no hope." I ignore her and trace my finger along what's left of the color map, along the path we're on, and figure, round-about, where we are.

"Here," I say, pointing.

Junko steps forward and motions to a large blue area on the map, north from where we are. There's no path headed in that direction, just the color green to indicate forest be-tween it and us. "And here is Saiko."

"Yeah, but no path going there. Not from here, anyway."

We both study the sign again, red Kanji scrawled along one side, the ominous warnings again reminding any who read it that they are loved and that they should turn back. It looks so far back to the parking lot where we started, and here we are, about half-way around the large loop of the main path. "I don't know what to tell you," I say. "I think we got on the wrong path."

"How is that?"

"I think when we were at the fork we must've gone the wrong way. See?" I point to the board again, showing her a small path mostly cut off from the broken sign and how it loops around near the lakeshore. "I'm sorry."

"There has to be another way."

"Not without backtracking the last few hours, and we don't have time for that," I say. "Say what you want, but we're not staying here after dark."

She ignores me. "I do not believe it. These woods . . . there are many paths. Many people visit here."

"None of this is for tourists," I say raising my hand and pointing to the surrounding woods, to the limp streamers of yellow tape hanging broken from the trees at intervals, warning us not to go any further, that there's nothing good ahead. "It's for people looking for bodies, like us. And those Suicide Squads or whatever. This isn't a national park, not like what you're thinking."

She ignores me and goes back to the sign, looking through the spray-painted graffiti, hoping to find some clairvoyance in the worn, splintered wood. "We have to try," she says finally.

"Try what?"

"If we cut through here, it is a short distance to the lake, yes?"

"In theory, yes, but there's no trail."

"I understand, but we . . . we could use those ribbons," she says excitedly, pulling on my arm. "And I promise to you, Bill, that we will go there, to the lake, and come right back. I just . . . need to see it, the water."

"I know, you've said that, but you don't know what we'll find, if anything."

She steps back and looks at me directly for what seems like the first time. "I understand that I may never find anything of hers. That . . . she is gone to me. I do understand that.

But at the very least I can make a *hokura* to her, a place I can come back to visit. I cannot come this far and do . . . nothing."

I look back to the sign, then at Junko: her lips full and red, inviting, her eyes pleading, beautiful, and for the first time in a long while I feel passion, I remember why I told her I would come with her in the first place. "If we do this," I say stepping toward her and running my hand through her hair, "then we have to use the ribbons, make sure we don't get lost."

"Yes," she says hugging me, arms slung around my neck. "Of course."

"And I'm serious. We get to the lake, you do what you have to, and then we leave, okay?"

"Yes, I understand. Thank you, Bill."

Junko kisses me on the lips and for a moment we fall into each other, pulling each other close, everything else disappearing around us until, a moment later, she comes to and pulls away from me, shy and nervous again. "Th-thank you," she says softly, looking away.

I pull the ribbons from my pack and separate them into pieces, counting off a handful and putting the rest away. We drink some water in silence as I study the sign again, wondering how long it will actually take to get to the lake from here. By the time we're ready we've been here for almost twenty minutes, preparing ourselves and figuring out exactly what our plan will be, deciding that she'll lead, me walking behind to place the ribbons. And as we make our way into the woods, for the first time since we've been here, I hear a bird call, a sweet whistle echo throughout the woods, and look up to see a lonely black bird flying overhead, almost like he's talking to us.

"Look," I say grabbing Junko's arm and motioning up. "That's the first animal we've seen since we've been here."

We watch it dance on the branches of a tree, sing some more, then fly away, still singing. "A good sign," she says.

"I hope so."

We start again toward the woods and make our way under a strand of yellow tape tied between two small trees, all noise of the outside world, the bird's song and the small breezes— everything, completely vanishing the moment we do, which is so jarring I have to catch my breath and remind myself that we haven't just crossed into some other dimension. I tie the first ribbon on a tree within sight of the large sign, making sure it's high enough so we can easily see it as we make our way back. I smile at Junko as I catch her looking at me.

"Are you ready?" she asks.

"I guess."

She leads us into the familiar landscape of jagged and toothy rocks, small inclines and valleys, through the endless gray-brown of the trees themselves, some with roots popped up and exploding in all directions, most of the trees thin, branches starting at the ground or halfway up making it, at times, hard to see too far ahead. We continue like that for about forty minutes and I tie a ribbon every fifty feet or so, making sure the previous one is still in eyesight. As we move I marvel at the quiet of the woods, how it blocks any and all noise out, and watch Junko, the scout on this part of the journey, staying steadily ahead of me, looking at everything, constantly searching and calculating.

"How are you feeling?"

"Fine, but maybe we can stop for some water?" Junko pauses, stretching her legs on two rocks into an a-frame, wiping her forehead clean. I can't help but look at her body, hungry.

"Sure."

I set my pack down and pull out my water bottle and drink. Junko does the same but quickly puts it away and begins looking around us, kneeling in areas and raking her hand through the fallen leaves, still looking for a some- thing. Anything. I sigh, loudly, probably an attempt to let her know I'm not nearly as amused as she is, but she doesn't hear me, or pay attention, I'm not sure which. I kick my shoes along the ground through a clump of leaves and somehow in the midst of my actions, kicking things in little piles, I uncover a small, black hairclip.

"Hey," I say picking it up and showing it to Junko. "I found a hairclip."

She rushes over and takes it from me, looking at it, her lips twisting into a smile, one of those a-ha smiles like things are starting to come together. "Izumi!" is all she says.

"What about her?"

She flips the hairclip around in her fingers, inspecting ev- ery side before answering me. "This was Izumi's hairclip!"

"Uh, how do you know that?"

"She always wore one just like this, since we were girls. I used to wear a white hairclip and she wore a black one. Always."

"Yeah, but you don't know that's hers."

"Why not? It is possible she came this way too."

"Sure, but I imagine black hairclips are really popular, though, right? I mean, this could belong to anyone."

"No, I am sure this was hers." Junko looks at me beaming, and then places the clip in her hair along her temple.

"What are you doing?" I ask, slightly disgusted.

"This is . . . this is a great discovery. I really think we are going to find more."

"I just don't think it's a good idea for you to put that in your hair. You really don't know—"

"It is hers, okay?" She turns away from me. "I believe she came this way, to the lake."

"But we're only here by accident, remember? Look, I'm all for helping you explore, but the chances of us finding her trail, the exact way she came . . . it's not likely."

"But I believe this is a sign. She wore the same clip."

"Yeah, but—"

"Can you agree it is at least possible we could find Izumi's path?"

"It's possible, I guess, but the chances are, like—"

"I understand, Bill, but it is possible. And of all the places we could be, we are on a path to the water, and that is where you found not just any hairclip, but the exact one she wore. Do you not see what I am saying? I believe . . . we are going in the right direction. That we will find more of her."

"Okay," I say quietly, slowly, starting to worry about Junko as she begins scanning the trees again, looking for more things that could be Izumi's but probably aren't. "But have you thought about what happens if we actually find her?"

"What do you mean?" she says turning back to me.

"I mean . . . her body."

"Oh, well, I have thought of it, yes. I would like," she says, losing herself in the thought, then, forcing a smile, awkward and nervous: "I have it all planned out."

I smile back and look at my watch: it's nearly six. "I wonder how much further. We should have been there by now." I look at Junko who's back to her scouting, looking at the forest around us. "Hey, did you hear me? I really think we need to think about our game plan—"

"Do you see that?" she asks, silencing me with a finger, staring ahead in our intended destination toward the lake.

I step forward so I'm in line with her and strain my eyes to look ahead, between the trees, to find anything that may seem out of place that would've stolen her attention. "See what?"

"I . . . see something, up ahead."

"See what?"

"A hand, I think."

I still can't tell where she's looking, but stand up straight, not wanting a repeat viewing of the man in blue from earlier. "Are you sure?"

"I think so, yes. Do you see it?"

She takes my hand and extends my finger in the direction she's looking. I struggle still and then, finally, I see it too: a white glove peeking out from the back of a tree, jutting out awkwardly, not naturally. "What the hell is that?"

"A person?"

"Wearing a glove?"

"Should we go see?"

"You want to?"

"This is not like last time, when I just . . . when I found it on accident. Besides, this is the way we are going, so we do not have a choice, right?"

"I guess, but we could go around, if you wanted."

"Maybe it is not a person. Maybe it is another clue."

"Maybe," I say, wary.

Junko grabs my hand before I can say anything else and we start moving again. As we grow closer, still approaching the tree in question from behind, we can make out more details and the glove itself looks comically large and I wonder if it's maybe just another shrine, a totem to someone's fallen lover or brother or friend. When we get to the tree, which is massive compared to most of the others around it, we circle it slowly, cautiously, until we see it: a child-sized doll nailed upside down to the trunk of a tree, one each through the legs and hands, arms outstretched like it's waiting for a hug, stuffed with straw that's leaking out through tears in its clothes, its porcelain face cracked in places, equal parts menacing and comical.

"Creepy," I say. Junko nods in agreement and we step back, processing everything. "What does it mean?"

I look at her and she seems as puzzled as I am, but still stays very calm, and perhaps sensing my unease takes me by the hand around the tree, looking for more clues. We find a small wooden sign nailed to the tree, a handwritten note painted on it. Junko reads it for me: "This is my suicide note. My name is Mikage Hidaka and I came here because there is nothing good in my life. Nothing good ever happened to me. If you find this, do not look for me. I am cursed." Junko touches the sign and looks up at me.

"A suicide note."

I go back around and look at the doll again, touching its face, wanting to understand the reason behind it. Junko looks along the ground near the tree, kicking some leaves away, probably hoping to find something else.

"I don't understand," I say, poking at the doll's face.

"What?"

"I guess I don't understand how someone could do this."

"With the doll?" She joins me now, looking at it, touching the hairclip every few seconds, making sure it's still there.

"Killing yourself. I mean, I know, you told me, and I get it, Japanese are very proud, but you have to have a certain mindset to come to these woods, all alone, and do something like that. I just . . . don't get it."

"Which is why people like you can never understand their pain."

"You mean us?"

"What?"

"Why people like *us*, right? Unless you're planning on offing yourself without telling me." I smile.

"That is not funny."

"Sorry."

Junko steps forward and touches the doll, sighing. "I know."

We stand like that for a few more minutes, the awkward-ness settling back between us, the moment of passion from earlier gone, until she suggests we start moving again. As we walk, side-by-side now, nothing but the sound of the leaves crunching under our steps, I get the nerve to ask her what I've been meaning to since she first told me about Izumi. "Why did she kill herself?"

Junko ignores me, not saying anything at first, then, qui-etly: "The ghosts that are out here, the *yurei*, we believe that, if you die suddenly or violently, like a suicide, that you be-come trapped."

"Sure, I think a lot of cultures believe something similar to that, with ghosts."

She touches a nearby tree, looks up at the leaves, runs her fingers over the bark as I stop to watch her. "They continue to exist as *yurei* because they have . . . conflict." She looks at me. "It is . . . not finished? I cannot think of the word."

"Unresolved?"

"Yes, unresolved," she says looking back to the tree, touch-ing it again. "So those who come to Aokigahara stay here with their secrets."

"What secrets?"

"Of life. Of what . . . makes them want to kill themselves. Secrets maybe only they know. And they can never rest be-cause they have never told anyone." She looks at me again and touches my hand. "And this is what keeps them here, lost to the world. The reason no one can help them."

"So what's keeping Izumi here?"

Junko drops my hand and I see there are tears in her eyes,

but she doesn't wipe them away. Instead she removes the hair-clip and fumbles it in her hands, between her fingers, playing with it, like a child. "I . . . can't, Bill."

"Can't what? Tell me?"

"I can't tell you her secret. I . . . made a promise, and that is all I have of her now."

"You promised you wouldn't tell her secret? Why she came here?" I say, then, not even waiting for an answer, add: "So you never told your parents?"

She looks confused and overwhelmed, her thoughts entangled, unsure how to respond. Then: "No one. We . . . made a pact together. And I promised her. It is the reason I am here. Why I needed to come, to help keep it." She buries herself in my chest. "But I am scared. These woods, everything, it is why I needed you here with me. To help me see it through."

"That's fine," I say pulling her close, my mind spinning, wondering what it all means. "I understand. You don't have to tell me anything, okay?"

"Okay," she says. I stop trying to think about everything, instead focusing on Junko, my beautiful Junko, crying and upset, losing it before my eyes, realizing just how strong she really is. She eventually peels herself from me sniffling, her eyes red and puffy, no smile this time. She takes the hairclip and slides it into her hair, pulling a few strands away from her face.

"It looks nice," I say.

"Thank you," she says looking at me, then almost through me, to the forest, distracted by all the possibilities of what it holds. All its secrets.

"Are you okay?" I try to hold her hand, to comfort her some more, but she pushes me off and takes a few steps back. She looks back into the trees, up our makeshift path, then crosses her arms.

"Let's go," she says slowly, biting her lip and moving away from me. "I bet the lake is just up ahead."

Shinji Yamada had only been to a sarakin once, as a child, the dirty neon signs and stained floors like something out of a movie forever etched in his mind. But, through an increasingly ugly series of circumstances—involving and not limited to his job, family, and less-than-ideal gambling debts—he found himself back again thirty years later. Shinji, a salaryman, had not yet told his wife that the promotion he was sure to get was awarded to another, and had been, for the past six months, staying in the city longer, sleeping in capsule hotels or even the train station so she would entertain the notion of his importance by this increasing absence. He also found himself drawn back to the tracks, feverishly betting at first a small sum on a horse of his choosing, then a week's salary, and finally, nearly a month's. At times he might pull ahead, or buy his wife and son nice things to appease any possible concerns, but soon things—as they often do—got worse. He could not pass by a pachinko machine without putting something in, and between that and the horses and even the illegal bets on baseball teams (his was the Tokyo Yakult Swallows), Shinji was now hundreds of thousands of dollars in debt.

So he found himself at the entrance to a sarakin one evening after work, a place he had promised himself he would never go, and, once inside, discovered it was not nearly as seedy as he had recalled from his childhood. There was a beautiful girl working behind the counter, and a well-meaning, handsome manager watching her every move, smiling at the customers as they made their requests. Once Shinji had made his, he was taken into a back room and was told, politely, that his request had been rejected—"The economy is not what it once was," was the reason given. He pleaded with them, and perhaps feeling sympathy for the man, the manager gave Shinji a phone number to call, an off-license lender that could, at least short-term, provide him with at least half of the sum he sought.

For two weeks he considered calling the number, ignoring the impulse to gamble. For a while it was fine, suppressed, but soon he found himself missing the smell of the track, the sounds of the pachinko, the roar of the baseball stadium when a player had made a hit. It had become too much to bear, and his wife—his beautiful wife—had begun to ask questions about his job, about the money coming in and why one of their credit cards had been declined. Shinji made the call and a man called Renzo answered, told him where to meet him to discuss further—a café in Kabukichō.

A day later Shinji and Renzo were discussing politics over coffee—as well as beautiful women that passed them by—and finally the loan itself.

"How much do you need?" Renzo said as he drank.

"Well, ideally . . . eight million Yen."

"Not possible," Renzo replied coldly, watching a pretty young girl enter the café. "I can give you two-point-five million today. Right now."

"But I need—"

"I do not care what you need. That is what I can offer at a rate of thirty percent to be paid back within ten days. Do you accept?"

Shinji drank, thought of his family. It wasn't enough to pay off his debts, but with one well-placed bet, he might be able to double—or even triple—the money in no time. "Yes, I accept."

"I thought you might."

Renzo took Shinji to a nearby apartment, a cramped and dingy-looking place used for his shady dealings. Renzo told Shinji to stay in the living room—where a child blissfully ignorant of his surroundings, Renzo's son, perhaps, watched cartoons.

"Wait here. I have to get a few things in the back."

Shinji joined the boy on the couch—oblivious to the stranger—and watched cartoons for nearly ten minutes. Renzo returned carrying a Daiei shopping bag and, not wanting to do business in front of the boy, took Shinji into the main hall.

"Take a look inside, if you want," Renzo said. "But first, give me your license."

Shinji did, and studied the money in the bag. "It is a lot of money."

"I know."

"Is there anything to sign?"

Renzo laughed. "No, nothing to sign. But—" He held up the license. "—I know you now. And if you do not pay this back in full in ten days, I will come after you. Believe me," Renzo leaned in for effect, "you do not want me coming after you. You or your family."

"I understand."

Later, in a more moderately-priced hotel—a splurge, he had told himself—Shinji sat on the bed, television and most of the lights turned off, violently flipping through a newspaper, stopping finally when he saw information about the races at the Tokyo Racecourse. He checked his watch and, determined to make the last race, bolted from the room, to a taxi, and emerged almost thirty minutes later at the towering structure.

Inside Shinji felt different—more powerful. He picked up the nearest racing form and scoured it for information, watching others like him and feeling, for the first time, superior. With the brick of money in his coat pocket he selected what he thought were sure bets. As he approached the teller—an automated machine could not be trusted with this sum—he had planned on making a few small bets, at least today, a few trifectas, perhaps even an exacta, but as he stood there, the young girl on the other side waiting for him to place his bet, the words slipped out on their own: "Pick six. Two-point-five million."

The girl processed the money with little regard for this man, and when she handed over the ticket, Shinji took it and held it like an infant—careful not to crumple or crease it on his trek to the stands. He didn't have to wait long—only another fifteen minutes for the race to start—but it felt like an eternity, and as every minute dragged on, he thought more and more of his wife, his family, and what would happen if he lost it. What would happen to them all. And then, it was a blur, the events of the next hour: the announcer coming on, greeting the crowd, the cheers and laughing from the happy people. The horses lining up for the first race, the sound of the gates opening. The sound of the horses' feet on the dirt. The excitement. His horse coming in last . . . dead last. And this repeated itself for five more races, his horse, the horse he picked, coming in either last itself or almost-last, never further up than that, the jeering from those who likewise lost, the people filing out, Shinji leaving and finding himself back in the hotel, alone, no money to even pay the room's fee for another night. Nothing.

The loss—the six losses—did not fully sink in until the next day, when he was at work. He vomited at his desk and was told to go home. His mind spun, his body had become numb, floating him everywhere, his feet inches off the ground, in a daze, completely oblivious to everything. Every idea he could think of, every scheme and notion that popped into his head in order to get the money back, was greeted ultimately with failure. He had no extended family he could ask for help—neither he nor his wife came from money—and he had no real friends he could confide in, not for something like this, anyway. So he watched the days tick away, unable to do anything, spending the time with his family while he could, watching them and crying when they were not looking, so as not to give away his predicament.

On the tenth day, still in a daze and unable to process the horrible truth, Renzo intercepted him after work near a restaurant he particularly liked.

"It is time, Shinji," Renzo said pulling him under the awning of the restaurant. "Should we go inside, get some food, and discuss?"

"I would prefer to stay out here," Shinji replied.

"Ah, yes, with all these people. Relax. I just want to know where we stand."

Shinji shifted in place, tightened the grip on his briefcase. "I . . . I do not have it."

"I assumed as much."

"You did?"

"When I saw you coming. The way you carried yourself. Not hard to detect, really. But I am sorry to hear that."

"Please," Shinji grabbed his shoulders, pleading, "Can I just have a few more days? I think there is a way that I may be able

to—"

"*Stop, stop,*" Renzo said. "*Just stop. What would a few days buy you? Not much, I think.*"

"*But my family . . . are you going to hurt them? Kill them? They have done nothing!*"

Renzo pulled out a cigarette and lit it, smiled at a girl that walked by. "*I could do that, yes, after I hurt you first, but there is an alternative, Shinji.*"

"*There is?*" *he said wiping his face clean.*

"*Yes, there is. Do you have life insurance?*"

"*Yes, I do.*"

"*And your wife and child—they are covered?*"

"*Yes.*"

"*And one final question: Does your life insurance cover suicide?*"

"*I believe so, yes.*"

"*That is good, Shinji. Very good. So here is what I propose to you: You will kill yourself. I do not care how, and I do not care where, so as long as you do it.*"

"*Kill myself?*"

"*I am not finished. You will kill yourself, and you will leave explicit instructions for your wife, once the money clears, to give me a sum of it, what is owed to me plus an additional ten percent inconvenience fee.*"

"*Inconvenience?*"

"*Yes. Thanks to you, now I will have to wait for all this to blow over before I get my money back. At any rate, that will cover your debts, and if you do this, I promise you no harm will come to your family. If you do not, though, that same promise no*" *longer applies. Do you understand?"*

Shinji stood there in shock until Renzo snapped his fingers, getting his attention. "Y-yes, I understand. I know what I have to do."

It was surprisingly easy for Shinji two days later to say good-bye to his family, leaving a note in his wife's jewelry box—where she would be sure to find it. He was sad, yes, but the notion that they would be taken care of and safe after his death got him through it. In deciding what to do and where to go he decided first to get as far away from his home as possible—he did not want his family to find him, ever, so he chose Aokigahara, and the method came simply to him then: pills and rope.

By the time he stepped in the woods he had taken his first two pills—his wife's prescriptions—and not even fifteen minutes later he took three more. An hour after arriving he began to see the faces of those he knew in the trunks of the trees, dancing along the branches and leaves, mocking him as they ought to. He wasn't sure how much time passed after that, when the last pill had been swallowed, but he managed to find a secluded area bordered by large stones, trees taking root atop, and thought, for the briefest of moments, that it was beautiful. With his senses dulled—an act of cowardice, he understood, but a necessary one to get him through it—he struggled to place the rope around a branch, tied tight around his neck. He then stood, prepared as he could be, looking at his arms, the neon blue of his parka, none of it seeming to belong to him, and without much else, no words spoken, only a hazy, veiled image of his family circling in his mind, he took a step forward and dropped sharply, wiggling and kicking in place until the life left him completely.

Sacrifice

"I think I hear the water," Junko says climbing up the rock ahead of me.

I stop in place, my hands clinging to the wall that seems to have come out of nowhere, jutting up from the forest floor and rising at a sharp enough angle to give us a true workout about twenty feet to what looks like a plateau. "I don't hear anything. I think we're lost."

Junko stops as well, looks back down to me. "That is why we have the ribbons."

"Well, we should've reached the lake by now."

She ignores me and keeps climbing, so I follow, making sure to put my feet in the right place, pulling myself up, my shirt drenched and clinging to my body. After another few minutes I see Junko disappear over the lip of the wall. I soon follow and pull myself up, finding the plateaus are nothing but more trees, more green and brown and gray in every direction. I see Junko up ahead some, standing in place, waiting and listening for a sign to tell her we're on the right track. I look back down the wall, at the forest, and see the last ribbon not far from it, then take another from my pack and tie it to the nearest tree, catching my breath as I do.

"So, where's the water?" I ask, annoyed.

"I thought I heard it."

"I told you, we're lost."

"Not lost."

"Clearly we are. We've probably walked in one big circle."

She turns toward me, equally annoyed. "How could we be in a circle if you are using the ribbons?"

"Look around us," I say, yelling now. "Everything looks the fucking same!"

"Do not yell at me."

"Then admit there's a chance we're lost. We're not exactly on a trail. We're just walking along, hoping to stumble onto something."

She thinks for a moment, looks into the forest again and points. "We should go this way."

"No. We're not going anywhere."

She turns back to me, her face twisted, scared. "What?"

"We've wasted a whole day on this trip, and I think it's time we head back."

"Then," she says, tears forming, "you can leave. I will meet you at the car."

"No, that's ridiculous. We'll go back together."

"I cannot leave."

"We have to. It's late," I say looking at my watch. "It's almost seven-thirty. It's going to get dark soon."

"If your time is so important to you, then I would rather not have you join me now," she says starting to walk off. "This was not about you or your time. This was about Izumi. This was about finding something of hers. This was about what she did and how she left things and how I will make them right."

I start after her. "I know why I came, Junko. I came because I care about you. All I've been trying to get you to admit is that there's a chance you may never find out what happened. That you may never find her at all."

"I will find her."

"Stop it, Junko," I say, running now, trying to catch up to her. When I reach her I can tell she's crying before she even turns around, but I don't say anything, I just grab her above the elbow and spin her toward me. She faces me, terrified, angry, then pulls away, back toward the woods. I grab her shoulder this time. "That's enough, all right?"

She keeps fighting me, pulling away, so I let her go, seeing how determined she is. "Do not touch me," she says between tears once she's far enough ahead of me.

"I'm sorry. I didn't mean to . . ." I stop.

"You are always sorry!" Junko stops and leans against a tree, looking out ahead. Nothing but quiet around us. I'm a few paces back still, likewise standing in place, waiting for her to do something. I take out one of the ribbons and tie it to a tree nearby.

"Why didn't you tell your parents you were coming here?" I ask.

"What?"

"Your parents. You told them we were going to visit the city."

"How do you know that?" she says walking back toward me, her arms folded up into her chest.

"I can speak some Japanese," I say. "I heard a few words, figured it out."

"Because they would have told me not to come, Bill. They would have told me to forget about her like they have."

"They haven't forgotten her, Junko."

"Yes, they have. They live as if she never was. As if it was just me and them. It . . . it makes me sick."

"I'm sure—"

Junko is right next to me now, in front of me, and before I can even finish my thought she pushes me hard, shoves me to the ground. "You do not know! Do you understand? You do not know everything!"

I prop myself up on my elbows now, studying her. "I know that. I'm not trying to say I do. I just . . . I'm asking is all. You never tell me anything, so what else can I do but ask and assume?"

Junko turns and stomps away letting out a frustrated scream. "It is not your business to know everything."

"Then why did you bring me here?"

Junko stops, facing away from me again, the view of her back familiar to me now. She's breathing heavy, shoulders rising up and down with every great breath she takes in and hisses back out. "There are things you cannot know. That you would not understand about Izumi and me. Our relationship."

I stand, keeping my distance. "Okay."

"My parents, when this happened, they were . . . I have never seen them like that. For days they did not speak. Not a single word. Then, after two weeks exactly, they put all pictures of her away. They refused to talk about her, about what had happened. They acted as if Izumi had never lived and took all their secrets to the grave with her."

"Their secrets?"

"Y-yes," she says, stuttering, nervous. "Anyway, then I left for university, away from them, but I never forgot. And I realized I needed to come here, to fulfill my promise to her. To keep her alive. And to show him he did not win."

"Show who?"

Junko turns back to me, wiping her eyes clean. "It does not matter. Izumi sacrificed much for me, protecting me from many horrible things she experienced. And coming here is what I need to do. If you cannot understand that, then there is not much left to say."

"I don't have any brothers or sisters," I say moving toward her. "So, you're right, it's hard, trying to understand this bond and what happened between you two. But I'm here because of you. You need to know that."

"I know."

She presses her hand against my cheek. "It won't be much longer, Bill. I promise." She smiles and walks away from me, leaving me standing there, watching her move through the trees like she belongs, a sense of purpose riddled through her movements now, and even though my brain's yelling at me to stop and turn back, my legs start up again and I find myself slowly following her deeper into the woods like I have no choice at all.

Kimiho's father Goro was nearly eighty when dementia had fully taken his mind. Some days were better than others, but on most he could hardly recognize his only daughter, who visited him at the nursing home out of obligation and little else. He would regale her with tales of his own father, a Kamikaze during the Pacific War, going on about honor and loyalty to the Empire of Japan. Kimiho had heard it all before, of course, but the intensity and ferocity at which he retold the tales again and again—details slightly altered as his brain could no longer recognize fact from fiction—never ceased to amaze her.

And it was near his eighty-first birthday when Kimiho began an affair with a coworker, someone whom she had been attracted to since her first weeks on the job. And she found herself visiting her father now for another reason: her lover Orito lived nearby, and since her husband could not stand the sight of her father, she knew there was no risk of him finding out.

The bi-monthly visits soon became weekly as her feelings for Orito became increasingly more complicated, due in part to a recent miscarriage—Orito's child, she was positive. And as the weeks dragged on and she saw the increasing strain on her marriage, the toll it took on her husband as he pined for her even though she snuck around behind him—he was, after all, an ideal husband, just lacking the virility she desired. She even began to blame her father, in his decrepit state, for making her this way, dissatisfied with a life that contained, as far as she could tell, everything she had ever asked for.

"Do you remember when you cheated on Mom," she asked her father one day.

"What?" Goro said looking first at her, then through her to

the back wall of his room. "Did Koyoshi come to see you? Did he tell you?"

"Dad, I am your daughter, Kimiho. Please, listen to me."

"Yes, Kimiho. What is it, my dear," he said holding a hand out. "Talk to me, please."

"You cheated on Mom when I was young. I remember. I was not supposed to find out, but I heard her on the phone one night with Mariko and she explained the entire thing."

"Mariko . . ."

"Yes, Dad, her sister. Anyway, I am—" Kimiho stopped and swallowed and even though she knew her father wouldn't remember what she told him five minutes from now, she seemed hesitant. "—I am having an affair. I never . . . I never wanted to do this. Dai is a good man. Very loving, and he supports us. But something is not there."

Goro had already diverted his attention to a nurse nearby handing out medication. "Very hard," he said. "You must be sure."

"No, listen. Please. How did you . . . This is your fault," she said finally. "Something happened . . . I saw how easy it was for you, desiring something other than us, and I think . . . I think you broke me."

Goro turned back to her slowly. "Not broken," he said. "Human."

It had been the first time Kimiho had mentioned her affair out loud, even to herself, and she stood, shaking. "I love Dai. Very much. Why do I keep doing this to him?"

"Human," Goro said. "Human human human."

Kimiho left and did not go back to visit her father for weeks, unable to look into his big, empty eyes, seeing herself in them. She tried, desperately, to fix things at home with Dai, spending more time with him and showering him with affection—and cutting herself off from Orito altogether—but the closer she got the more he pulled away. And then, seemingly out of nowhere, over dinner at home, Dai asked her: "How long have you been seeing him?"

"Seeing who?" Kimiho asked. "What are you talking about?"

"Please just . . . stop. I am not stupid."

"I really do not understand—"

"That man, from your work. Orito, was it? He came by here ten days ago looking for you. He had no idea you were married, or that I was your husband. He told me everything."

"Dai, listen—"

"No, just stop. He told me . . . that you saw him after you saw your father. That you only went to see him so you could . . . meet up."

Kimiho's heart and mind sped up. "I did see my father," she said finally, quietly.

"And then Orito?"

"Yes."

Dai stood, wiping his face. "How could you do this? What have I done to you?"

"Nothing! You have been perfect, Dai! This is . . . my fault. It is . . . my father's fault!"

"Your father? Are you joking? His brain is a pile of mush. He does not even know what year it is."

Dai turned to leave but Kimiho stopped him. "He cheated on my mom when I was little. I . . . it messed with my head."

"Do not blame him. He did not do this to me. You did."

Dai shook her hand free, grabbed his coat and left. Kimiho did not stop him, nor did she want to: he was right. This was her fault, not her father's.

The following weeks were dreadful, and again Kimiho found herself visiting her father frequently, the only person who would give her company—not even Orito would talk with her, nor anyone else from the office once he had told them about her. She found some solace listening to Goro drone on and on, but eventually even that could not better the sick feeling that rose in her throat at the thought of her husband, the man she had promised to be good to, not being able to stand the sight of her. She lost ten pounds in under three weeks, her appetite fading fast, and while Dai had not asked her to move out, not even mentioned the word divorce, what they had now was far worse—ghosts living in the same home.

Then, after it had seemingly been like this forever, Dai finally relented: "I am going to stay with my brother for a little while, to figure out what to do here. I think it is best for both of us."

Alone in their house, taunted by their memories, Kimiho felt even more alone than she ever had—her friends who at first stood by her side could no longer argue against her actions and how she had affected Dai. When she went to visit her father not soon after, she told him what had happened.

"And I do not know what to do," she said. "I am afraid he will leave me for good. But if he stays, if we work it out, I am afraid he will not be able to look at me the same ever again. I need your advice."

"Have you seen the Americans?" he said. "They are everywhere."

"There are no Americans here," Kimiho said wiping her tears away. "Just us. Now please, tell me what to do."

Goro touched her face. "My father met Emperor Showa. Did I tell you that?"

Kimiho smiled. "Yes, you did."

"My father was Kamikaze and killed many Americans. We were all so proud."

"That was a long time ago."

"He did it for honor. He sacrificed himself so we all would have a chance to live on. It was very brave."

They were interrupted by the nurse with the medication, and as Kimiho returned home later, her father's words echoed in her mind. She saw pictures of her and Dai—in happier times—and even tried to contact him but he would not answer. "For the best," she thought. She left a message, professing her love, telling him that she would fix this and that he would, someday, somehow, be better off without her.

Kimiho then picked out the same outfit she wore on the day she and Dai first met, and rummaged around in her father's old things they had held on to until she found it: her grandfather's Nambu pistol, still in working condition after all these years, meticulously cleaned and cared for by her father. It was easy enough to figure out, and her father—not one to throw any artifact of history away—had stashed a few stray bullets in a pile of belongings from the days of the Pacific War, more of his father's things. It took her almost no time to learn how to load the bullets as she wondered if her grandfather had ever killed anyone with it, or if she would be the first.

The next morning Kimiho took her car and drove to see her

Father, but could not—he had an especially bad night and was in a medically-induced sleep. She told the nurse to tell him thank you, then found herself on the road to Aokigahara—not wanting to bloody up anything in their house, so Dai could go on living in it after she was gone. She parked the car and tucked the gun—still loaded—into her purse in case any day hikers or passersby might be present. The woods were quiet and beautiful, and she enjoyed smelling the sweet fresh air. But it was short lived: she could not escape the thought of Dai, of what she had done, of her now-sullied marriage and the fact there was no way back.

She hiked another thirty minutes into the woods, assured she was now alone, stopping near a small shrine someone had erected to the memory of a loved one, someone else who had died sometime before, and Kimiho wondered if anyone would erect one in her honor—but figured probably not. She walked away from the path directly into the woods then kneeled and emptied the belongings of her purse onto the ground and sorted through them: make-up she never wore for Dai, a phone she used to use to call Orito with, various trinkets that reminded her of how horrible she had been, then: the gun. She picked it up and felt the weight of it and imagined her grandfather in the cramped cockpit, the great whirring of the jet engines surrounding him as he flew to his death in order to protect his country—his family. Kimiho then placed the pistol in her mouth, the barrel cold on her tongue, and thought only of Dai's smiling face on their wedding day as she pulled the trigger.

Enlightenment

I'm counting the ribbons and we only have a dozen left, crumpled and sweaty in my palm. I'm standing on top of a small hill and as I put the ribbons back in my pack I look down at Junko sitting on a tree stump at the bottom, listening to her headphones, oblivious to everything. I look back into the woods at the crest I'm on which again seems to plateau out, noticing that the scenery has changed some, the trees smaller here, younger maybe, fewer dried leaves on the ground and, if possible, even more green everywhere. To my left there's a large blue-green bush with orange berries on it, and for a moment I wonder if they're poisonous, but decide not to risk it, hungry or not.

"Junko!" I yell down to her but she doesn't hear me. I make my way down the hill slowly at first, between trees, over rocks and stumps, picking up speed as I make my way down, the breeze feeling good on me, when I suddenly hit a tree root and stumble to the ground into a somersault, rolling the rest of the way down through brambles, sticks and small green plants until I land on the ground about ten feet from her. When she sees me she rushes over and tries to help me up, but when I put weight on my left ankle the pain is so much that I collapse back to the ground, hammering the dirt with my fists.

"Your ankle?"

"Yeah, I twisted it."

"Does it hurt very much?"

"Well, I can't stand. So, yeah."

She kneels and touches it, softly. "Here?"

"Yeah." I wince and take off my backpack, lying back on the ground while she continues to rub the spot. Then she leans forward and touches my face.

"You are cut."

I touch the spot with my fingers and see a small amount of blood on the tips, my cheek stinging now. "I guess I hit a stick or something on my way down."

"Oh," she says pulling back and standing. "What did you find up there?"

"Nothing."

"No water?"

"There's nothing but trees," I say sitting up. "Just trees. No water. No lake. Nothing."

"That is very odd. What time is it?"

I look at my watch. "Eight-thirty."

"It is getting late."

"Yes, and if we don't get back to the main path soon we're going to be camping out in the woods."

She smiles at me then turns and steps toward the hill like she's ignoring my warning, like it doesn't mean a thing to her. I lay my head back and try to get comfortable, looking up at the twisted canopy, interlocking branches and blankets of leaves from a variety of trees shielding most of the sky from us, only pockets of gray visible here and there. I look back at Junko and she's already up the hill some, looking alternately at the ground I stumbled down and the trees I hit as I rolled.

"Where are you going?"

"Looking," she says. "Just looking."

"For what?"

"For anything."

"You're not going to find anything," I say propping myself up again, watching her slender legs move with great purpose.

"You never know," she says, stops, then squeals excitedly, letting out a giggle like I've never heard before.

"What? What is it?"

She kneels and comes up, holding something small and brown in her hand, too far away from me to tell what it is. "Do you see this?"

"No. Bring it here."

She's facing me now, smiling ear-to-ear, just beaming, carefully traipsing down the hill. When she reaches me she kneels and hands me a small clump of what looks like finely-shredded bark. "Do you see?" she says.

"I don't understand."

"This is a piece of the stuffed bear. Izumi's stuffed bear!"

I look at the brown lump again, inspecting it closer, thinking maybe, however doubtfully, it could be a dirty clump of brown fur. But probably not. "I don't think this is anything."

She grabs it from me and stands, stroking it. "Yes, it is. It is a piece of it. I believe . . ." she stops, looks toward the hill again. "Something is telling me she went up the hill. Out of all the places we could have been, we found her trail!"

"Junko, you need to stop."

"This means that out of all the places we could have been, and Izumi could have been, we found her trail. Do you understand? This is great news." She's admiring the clump again, almost giddy, truly believing that we've accomplished something here. "It is very clear to me now."

"Just stop, okay?"

"Stop?" She turns back to me, glaring. "Stop what?"

"That is nothing. It's a piece of bark or something."

"No, I understand now that—"

"It isn't a piece of fur, okay? You want it to be, just like you want that hairclip to be hers too, but it's not. None of this is."

She touches the hairclip at my mentioning of it then tucks the brown clump close to her chest. "It is hers. And I think the water is just up the hill. You did not look hard enough."

"I'm pretty sure I'd be able to see a big lake."

"You did not go far enough. You do not really care about finding anything. Admit it."

"At this point, all I care about is leaving these fucking woods."

"I knew it," she says. "I just knew it."

"Jesus Christ, what is wrong with you?" I force myself to get up, slowly, putting almost no pressure on my hurt ankle, supporting myself with a nearby tree.

"Nothing is wrong with me. You are . . . very selfish."

"How am I selfish? I'm here, aren't I? I've entertained this ridiculous notion long enough, right? What else do you want me to do?"

"To understand."

"Well, I'm sorry. I just can't. This is all way out of control and we are leaving."

"No." She turns back toward the hill and starts, but as she does I reach out and grab her arm again. She pulls away, hard, knocking me back. "Do not touch me!"

I trip but manage to keep myself standing on one leg. "Why are you fighting me like this?"

She looks at me but doesn't say anything, just turns back toward the hill and starts again. I reach out, intending only to stop her, but fall forward as I grab her backpack this time, putting all my weight into it and pulling her to the ground. She lands, hard, and screams as my weight crushes her tiny frame, hitting me repeatedly and yelling in Japanese words I don't understand. I finally manage to roll off, breathing heavy and lying on the ground again. She stands and looks at me, then realizes she dropped the clump of fur or whatever and panics, scrambling to her knees, searching until she finds it again. "I cannot believe you would attack me," she says.

"I didn't. I fell."

"No, you will do anything to stop me. You are like my parents. You can never understand Izumi and me." She starts up the hill.

"Where are you going?"

"Finishing this," she says without looking back.

"You're just going to leave me here?"

"Go home, Bill."

"Junko, stop." She doesn't say anything this time, just keeps hiking the hill, getting further away. My head drops back to the ground and I look back up at the canopy again, noticing it's gotten darker in the last few minutes. I try to pull myself up but the pain is worse now. After another moment of resting I manage to get up on my good leg and look up to see Junko half-way up the hill, still trudging ahead and not looking back, not seeming to care what happens to me. "Fuck."

I hobble toward the hill, only barely touching my bad foot to the ground, grimacing with every step. I drop to my knees and decide to crawl up the hill, watching her ahead of me, following her lead as I pull myself up and finding it much easier to move like this. I stop every so often to catch my breath, feeling like she's getting further away and I won't catch up at all. And suddenly I'm remembering how we met on campus, running into her as she was handing out fliers for some sort of research project she was working on with some other psychology students. I only went so I could see her, talk to her some more. And I remember how awkward our first date was, but how we seemed to just click after, how everything just seemed to be . . . right.

I look back up the hill, equally confused and distraught by the events, and watch as she disappears over the crest, out of sight. "Junko?" I wait a minute and don't hear anything back so I start moving faster, as best I can.

Then, after a few more paces forward, my hands raw from pulling myself along, I hear her: "Bill!"

"Junko? What is it? Are you okay?"

I start crawling again and stop as Junko appears at the crest of the hill, looking down at me and waving her arms excitedly. "I . . . saw something," she says. "A light, almost like a figure. I think it was her."

"Her?"

"Izumi. She moved up ahead, into the woods."

I freeze. "What do you mean?"

"I saw something, I think it was her. I think . . . she's telling me to come and follow her."

"Junko, you need to stop. Wait for me."

She smiles at me from the top of the hill and blows me a kiss. "I have to go now."

"Junko?" I ask, still frozen in place, alarmed by this, watching as she gives me a final look then disappears over the hill.

I crawl faster now, the pain in my ankle dulled, my head spinning as I try to figure out what's going on. By the time I reach the top I stand, slowly, looking around, but don't see Junko anywhere. "Hello?" I look back down the hill then to the pieces of sky breaking through the trees and realize it's already past dusk, my eyes adjusting to the quickly spreading darkness. I don't hear anything, don't see any way she could have gone.

Then, amidst the quiet, I hear her shout: "The water, Bill! I hear the water!"

I move forward then stop, realizing I need to put ribbons in place, even if it's going to get dark soon. My hands are shaking as I take my pack off and I notice it's already open. I rummage for the ribbons and don't find them and figure my pack must've unzipped when I fell on Junko, when she struggled to get me off her. I hobble back to the hill and look down, squinting to see: near the bottom, the small stack of yellow ribbons smiles at me, lying in stark contrast to the dark forest floor.

I take a step toward the hill and feel a jolt of pain in my

swollen ankle, the pain moving up my leg from all the pressure I've put on it. I look back to the woods, unsure of what to do, realizing there's not enough time to get the ribbons *and* find Junko. As I stand here contemplating, I hear her voice once again, quieter now, further away.

"I'm coming!" I zip up my pack and even though I know I should just stay and wait here until morning, I take a large step forward and limp in the direction of Junko's voice.

Isi and Huyu could not believe such a book existed—an entire manual devoted to the methods and means of suicide—and even more so, they could not believe such a book was readily available to buy. But once they had it the two boys became obsessed with it, with what it preached—that suicide was noble, even honorable, something not to be looked down upon at all, an individual choice that was neither illegal nor against any national religion in Japan. Initially it was the draw of the macabre that danced in their heads—for instance, they had no idea before reading the book that there were so many different means of suicide—but the more they read on the internet, the more curious they became. They would meet at one another's homes after school and research feverishly, discovering the existence of internet suicide cults: groups of people that would commit suicide together, advocating that it did not have to be a solitary act at all, but something shared by like-minded individuals. Even more intriguing was that some people were adamant that group suicides presented a sort of illumination at the very end of life, before it was all over, that was otherwise impossible to experience in the world.

The boys weren't particularly lonely or depressed, but they were bored, so this new passion of theirs took a hold of their lives above all else. As they built their courage they would print articles of group suicides that had been successful—most recently, nine found dead of carbon monoxide poisoning in a van—analyzing what went right and what went wrong, consulting the suicide manual to determine which method would be the most ideal. They joined chatrooms and talked to others like them that had become enamored with this idea, discussing alternative means and the most ideal locations, finding many were as young as them, if not younger. It became to these cultists less about the need to end their lives and more of an ideology, something their parents and elders and the generations before them could never understand, the most exclusive of clubs—and that, in itself, was reason enough to entertain such notions.

The more they prepared and talked with their new friends— who they oftentimes were invited to join, but declined out of fear, as they were not quite yet ready—the more they withdrew themselves from the real world. Finally, after an online friend of theirs—a girl who called herself Coco—joined a group who died by charcoal burner, the boys decided it was their time to join those who had gone bravely before. So they split their tasks—Isi would take his mother's sleeping medication while Huyu would find plastic bags—and they left the watchful eye of their friends and families and their well-to-do neighborhoods to head for Aokigahara where they could die in peace, uninterrupted in order to fully experience the enlightenment. They had had many offers, almost daily, to join other groups—one in particular that same day, again with charcoal burners, was especially appealing—but the boys wanted to limit any outside factors that could, similarly, prevent them from going through with it. They sent their goodbye messages to their online friends via their phones, all of which were greeted with enthusiasm or jealousy in being strong enough to do it, to be part of this righteous cause, and when they arrived finally at Aokigahara, so proud of themselves and what they would do, they practically beamed.

In the forest they began taking Isi's mother's pills in order to dull their reflexes, and marched through the dark woods with great resolve and purpose until their eyes grew heavy and they knew it was time. They picked a spot and sat cross-legged, across from one another, giggling and talking about what they expected to find on the other side, how great it would be to join their friends and be a part of something so wonderful, and, as night fell, they placed plastic bags on the other's head, holding it tight at the end, promising each other they would never let go and finding the strength in one another they knew they would not have individually.

Blackness soon came to them and took them over and they struggled some, naturally, trying to remove the other's hand from around the end of the plastic, weak from the pills and unable to do anything, their eyes never straying from one another, looking out onto the world through the foggy plastic as they had never seen it before.

Freedom

Night comes fast and I can barely see anything now: some bluish light from the moon shining between bare patches of the treescape and not much else. I stop and fish around in my pack for the tiny flashlight we picked up at a convenience store on a whim, one of those ones that clips onto your keychain. I find it and turn it on, searching the woods immediately in front of me, and find nothing but more trees and craggy, uneven earth again. "Junko!" I say again, louder this time. Still nothing. I start forward, my ankle swollen twice its normal size now, and lean against another tree as I stop to catch my bearings. I wait and listen, realizing I've never been so alone in a place so quiet, but my nerves, the worry I have for Junko, finding her in this maze, all of that masks any sort of fear I'd otherwise be feeling.

"Can you hear me?" I call again, moving forward slowly. "My ankle hurts really bad, and . . . I'm scared, Junko." I pause. "Hello? Can you hear me?"

I move again, faster now, headed in what I think is a straight line, but I can't be sure. I move past a row of very thin trees and down a small embankment, over some sort of small creek, the only water we've seen so far. I stop to study it, watching as it disappears in both directions into the blackness. It barely makes a noise as if it's been muted like everything else here. On the other side I manage to climb back up from the water and hear a bird cry again. I jump and shine the flashlight up into the trees and can't tell if it's the same bird as before, or if it's even a bird at all, so I continue again, still looking for whatever made that noise, unaware the forest floor suddenly drops off. I lose my footing and fall hard, on a succession of rocks, screaming mostly out of fright, until I land on a patch of cold dirt. I blink myself into cohesion, flashlight still in-hand, and shine it around—I'm in some sort of small riverbed, bigger than the creek from before, the opposite bank so steep that I hurt just thinking about climbing out. I manage to stand and find cuts on my hands and arms as I brush myself off, all of them stinging now in harmony.

Along the lip of the opposing bank I see nothing but a series of thick and tangled trees, branches spreading from the bases, and I wonder how I'll force my way through once I get up there. And then, out of nowhere, I see Junko, standing between the trees, only the light from my flashlight and the tiniest glimmer from the moon illuminating her: her back is facing me and she starts laughing, that odd giggle again. When I see her, when I realize what I'm looking at, I jump back, nearly falling but catching myself before I do.

"Junko!"

"She is so beautiful," she says quietly, running a hand through her hair, still facing away.

"Are you okay? I've been looking for you."

"I missed you," she says, then disappears into the trees.

"No, don't go . . . ," I say, walking slowly toward the other side of the riverbed, realizing she's gone again. "Fuck, fuck."

I hobble over and up the bank and hike up, finding a

less cluttered section of trees at the top that I force my way through. "Junko?" Nothing. I move forward, slowly, my feet silent. I stop and realize this part of the woods smells different, more fragrant. Up ahead I see the tree line thinning out so I keep moving, my breathing hard, the flashlight going all over the place, finding it difficult to keep it steady. After another ten minutes I spill out into a clearing overlooking a large black lake: Saiko.

I'm in awe of the size of it, and in the distance, beyond the lake, I can see the top of Mt. Fuji, capped in white even in the dark of night. A beacon. I can't help but smile that even after everything, we actually did find the water. But my smile breaks when I see Junko again, standing at the edge of the overlook, which, from what I can tell, shoots straight down to the water below. She's holding her backpack in her hand. It's the first time she hasn't been wearing it since we arrived this morning.

I step toward her. "You were right. We found the water."

"It is very beautiful, even in the night." She turns her head slightly, looking back at me over her shoulder, her face blank. "Thank you for coming with me today, Bill."

"Yeah, of course." I pocket the flashlight, the moon brighter here without the tree canopy keeping it from reaching us. My hands start shaking from the cold of the night and I clench my fingers into fists every so often to keep them working properly. "Are you okay?"

"Mhm," she says turning back toward the lake.

"I really am sorry about everything today." Silence. I take a few steps toward her and feel my ankle throb again, the pain shooting up my leg. I stop and look at the backpack in Junko's hand. "Are you going to make a shrine here?"

"I can hear her in the woods," she says.

"What do you mean?" I step closer. "Maybe you should move away from the edge. It looks like a long fall."

"I can see that this is where she spent her time. At the end."

"How do you know?"

She touches the clip still in her hair. "And now . . . we will be together."

"What do you mean? What are you talking about? Please, can you step back a bit? You're making me nervous."

I'm close enough that I could, if I wanted, reach out and touch her. I don't and I'm not sure why. "Please do not come any closer," she says.

"Fine, sorry." I pause. "We might not be able to find our way back tonight. We will have to sleep here." I take a few steps back, giving her space. "Is that okay with you? I can help you build the hokura . . . if you want."

She looks back at me, over her shoulder again, smiling like she did when we had our first kiss . . . a lifetime ago. "Thank you."

"Of course. Anything."

We stand there some more in silence, wind whispering on the water of Saiko, the waves dancing back and forth. Then I hear the bird again, at least what I think is the same bird that's been following us.

I look up and see dark clouds swirling in the sky and when I look back at Junko she has her hand in the backpack. After a moment she pulls something out: a book. "What is that?" I stumble toward her as she drops the backpack at her feet.

"These were her last words. I found them, in our hiding place," she says slowly, setting the backpack at her feet.

"Her words?"

"Details of what happened to us. She wants me to show the world," she says. "She wants them all to know."

"Know what?"

She's breathing heavy now and turns and looks at me, smiling. "I see her. All around us."

"Okay," I say, pleading as she tiptoes closer to the edge. "Please don't do anything crazy. You have a full life ahead of you, and Izumi would have wanted—"

"I love you," she says trembling, looking back out at the lake, then, in a flash, she throws the book to the ground and leaps straight out.

I stand there dumbfounded: it's like everything's in slow motion as Junko's body disappears over the lip. My body finally wakes up and I rush to the edge, calling out to her, searching through the darkness. There's no response and I wait to hear the sound of impact but there isn't anything . . . there's nothing. "Junko!" I cry out, and for a moment I think of going after her but can't move, my body frozen. I finally collapse backwards to the ground, watching the sky again, and in disbelief every small detail of the day races through my head, playing back and haunting me as I try to figure out if I should've known this could happen. If there was anything I could've done.

And I lie there like that for a while, holding onto the book now, a journal, repeating Junko's name over and over and feeling truly afraid for the first time today, looking out at Saiko spread in front of me, then at the woods behind—at Aokigahara—the way home swallowed up by trees and darkness.

Izumi Hayashi had started a journal when she was ten years old, filling it with dreams she had or things she wanted that she saw on television. But when she turned thirteen the contents of the book became darker, more sinister, the cause of which seemed to point to one night when her Uncle Naoki—her father's brother—came into her bedroom after a night of heavy drinking. Her father, a very proud man, had pieced together what had happened sometime later—made assumptions, really, based on previous lascivious behaviors—but did nothing about it except to make Izumi, his oldest daughter, feel as if she herself had done something wrong. That night changed everything for them, and Izumi's younger sister Junko—four years younger and naively unaware that anything at all had happened—was taken under her older sister's protection to ensure nothing like that would ever happen again to either of them.

As Izumi grew older she had no outlet but her pink journal, recording in detail everything that happened to her that night, including the frequent vivid dreams since which had caused her to relive it. "A single night," she couldn't help think. "A single night changed who we all are completely." Despite this she became a beautiful young woman, and her parents, either by sheer will or ignorance, seemed not to understand why she had withdrawn from them so. Boys and men alike threw themselves at her, and while she entertained some of them—sneaking off or even bringing them home when she knew she would have the house to herself—nothing could ever make her forget what had happened.

After university, Izumi got a job at a travel agency where she dreamed of whisking herself somewhere far away, believing that to be the only way she could truly move on from that night. But as she would plan, investigating hostels and hotels and even considering what she could do for work, she was reminded that she had a more immediate purpose—protecting Junko—and she would watch as the planning, however brief, would fall apart. But she harbored no regret for her choice to stay behind, that truly, she was unable to leave Junko alone for fear that something, anything, would happen to her—she figured, after all, at least she could be normal . . . could be happy—and after years of dashed inhibitions and broken promises to herself, she saw it her new mission to get her sister as far away from home as possible.

So Izumi pushed Junko to study hard and go to school in America—to see the world and leave them all far behind. Junko happily obliged her sister's fanciful wishes and notions, if nothing else than to distance herself from a cruel mother and a distant father, making Izumi promise that she would visit often. Junko never knew the real reason her sister pushed her to leave, nor could she see what Izumi had hidden behind her flawless façade by the time she had left—an addiction to Valium, a dependence on alcohol to just sleep fully through the night. And Izumi, far away from her younger sister, her only buffer from the horrible memories of her past, sank deeper down into a state of despair she could see no escape from.

Izumi tried hard those first few months after Junko left to live her life and to try to achieve some sort of normalcy—even taking a boyfriend for a short while, Yuu, a handsome young salaryman. But no matter what she did or how she tried to be normal, she found herself coming to the same inevitable conclusion: with Junko gone, and safe, she had served her purpose in this life. She tried for a time reliving her glamorous runaway plans, going somewhere foreign, far away, letting her past go completely, but the fire that was in her once seemed impossible to rekindle—a lifetime of looking over her shoulder, reliving the past the way she had and assuring it would not happen again had left her empty inside, devoid of luxuries such as daydreams. So Izumi further spiraled into a pit of dependencies—including more frequent experimentation with heroin—writing people off, and deciding, after months of trying, that there no longer was a point to it all. At least, she figured, with Junko now a woman, safe from ever having to suffer the way she had, she had accomplished something.

She wasn't quite sure when she had decided to end her life, when the last straw had been placed on her back, but it didn't matter, really—now that the seed had been planted, it was going to happen—so she planned the best she could for such a thing and decided to wait two days for Junko's birthday. The day soon came and she managed to get in touch with her beloved sister— the first time they had talked in weeks—but their conversation was short: Junko had met a boy, seemed happy, and was going out to meet him. She had no idea it would be their last conversation, but Izumi much preferred it that way, preferred knowing her sister was happy, and wouldn't have changed a thing. The next day she thought briefly of calling her mother and father but decided against it since conversations between them, at least in any formal way, hadn't existed in years. Instead she wrote in her diary one last time, a note for Junko, knowing no one besides her would be bothered to read her entries—would care to understand her—thanking her, telling her not to worry and that, truly, this was the best course of action. She then set out for Aokigahara by bus—her family had taken a trip there a year before the night that changed everything, when they were actually happy, deciding it would be a fitting location, a portal into what could have been only if things had worked out differently. If only that day had been erased altogether.

As she entered Aokigahara just after sunset, Izumi had no idea that her final words would inspire her sister sometime later to look for her, that what had happened to her so many years before—and the inability of her parents to do a thing about it—would affect her so profoundly. The bond she and Junko shared ran deeper than she would ever know, and as she disappeared into the woods, her thoughts dwelled on her sister, not of herself, hoping, above all else, that they would be together again someday.

About the Author

Robert James Russell lives in Ann Arbor, Michigan, and has known he wanted to be a writer since he was ten years old. A fan of well-placed stream of consciousness and stories that feature everyday characters and dialogue, Robert has a penchant for  stories focusing on relationships in all their many forms. In 2010, he co-founded the literary journal *Midwestern Gothic*, which aims to catalog the very best fiction of the Midwestern United States—an area he believes is ripe with its own mythologies and tall tales, yet often overlooked.

Follow Robert:
robertjamesrussell.com
midwestgothic.com
Twitter: twitter.com/robhollywood

Facebook: http://www.facebook.com/RobertJamesRussell. Author

ONE BIRD – ONE CAGE – ONE FLIGHT

An interpretation, in verse, of themes and images
from the letters of Emily Dickinson

Emily as a student at Mount Holyoke Seminary.
Photo taken in late 1847 or early 1848.
(*Photo courtesy Amherst College Library.*)

ONE BIRD - ONE CAGE - ONE FLIGHT

Homage to Emily Dickinson

by
ROGER WHITE

One is a dainty sum! One bird, one cage, one flight;
one song in those far woods, as yet suspected by
faith only!

Emily Dickinson

Naturegraph Publishers, Inc.
Happy Camp, CA 96039

Library of Congress Cataloging in Publication Data

White, Roger, 1929-
    One bird—one cage—one flight.

    "An interpretation, in verse, of themes and images from the
letters of Emily Dickinson"—P.
    1. Dickinson, Emily, 1830-1886, in fiction, drama, poetry,
etc. I. Dickinson, Emily, 1830-1886.
II. Title.
PR9199.3.W45305   1983   811'.54   83-22119

ISBN 0-87961-141-3, paperback
ISBN 0-87961-140-5, cloth

Naturegraph Publishers, Inc.
P. O. Box 1075
Happy Camp, California
96039

FOR THE BELLE OF AMHERST

and all my Emilys

Acknowledgements

Permission to use copyright material is gratefully acknowledged to the following:

The Association for Bahá'í Studies in the pages of whose tenth volume some of these poems first appeared; The National Spiritual Assembly of the Bahá'ís of the United States for extracts from *The Hidden Words of Bahá'u'lláh;* Louise Bernikow for extracts from "Emily Dickinson" in *The World Split Open,* London, 1974; John Malcolm Brinnin for extracts from "Emily Dickinson," edited by Richard Wilbur, The Laurel Poetry Series, New York, 1960; Columbia University Press for extracts from the entry for Emily Dickinson, *The New Columbia Encyclopedia,* New York and London, 4th ed. 1975; the President and Fellows of Harvard College for epigraphs attributed to Emily Dickinson from *The Letters of Emily Dickinson,* edited by Thomas H. Johnson, Cambridge, Mass., published by the Belknap Press of Harvard University Press, © 1958 by the President and Fellows of Harvard College; Daniel G. Hoffman for extracts from "Emily Dickinson" in *American Poetry and Poetics,* New York, 1962; Peter Jones for extracts from "Emily Dickinson" in *An Introduction to Fifty American Poets,* London, 1979; Jay Leyda for extracts from *The Years and Hours of Emily Dickinson,* two volumes, New Haven, Yale University Press, reprinted Hamden, Conn., Archon Books, 1970; Detroit Public Library for extracts from the letters of Margaret Maher contained in the Boltwood Family Manuscripts, used by courtesy of the Burton Historical Collection; Rollo May for an extract from *The Courage to Create,* New York, 1975; Vivian R. Pollak for extracts from "Thirst and Starvation in Emily Dickinson's Poetry" in *American Literature,* vol. 51, no. 1, March 1979; John Wain for extracts from "Homage to Emily Dickinson" in *Professing Poetry,* New York, 1977; Middlesex, 1978.

CONTENTS

PART TWO, Summer Song 1860-1869

EPILOGUE

AUTHOR'S NOTE

These poems in homage to Emily Dickinson were suggested by themes and images in her letters. Although their writing brought its own recompense of pleasure, I shall feel doubly rewarded if they awaken in the reader a virgin or renewed interest in the life and art of a great poet whose unsurpassed gift of articulating the spiritual promptings and misgivings that characterize the human condition will surely recommend her afresh to each succeeding generation as a contemporary.

DRAMATIS PERSONAE

THE FAMILY

EDWARD DICKINSON 1803-1874

Edward Dickinson was born in Amherst, a quiet village in the Connecticut Valley of Massachusetts about 100 miles from Cambridge and Concord and, at that time, lacking considerably their pace and sophistication. He was a patriarch of the Puritan tradition—dominant, stern, remote and awesome. His heart was "pure and terrible," Emily said and on Sundays he read "lonely and rigorous books"; but he was never heard to "utter a harsh word" and he commanded the respect and affection of his wife and children to the end. He died on June 16, 1874, while visiting Boston. He was the leading lawyer of Amherst and in later life treasurer of Amherst College and a member of the legislature and of Congress. His daughter, Lavinia, it was reported, said of him, "Father never kissed us goodnight in our lives. He would have died for us, but he would have died before he would let us know it."

EMILY (NORCROSS) DICKINSON 1804-1882

Before her marriage to Edward Dickinson on May 6, 1828, Emily Norcross lived in Monson, Massachusetts. After their marriage they lived on Main Street in Amherst in "one of those large, square brick mansions so familiar in our older New England towns, surrounded by trees and blossoming shrubs without, and within exquisitely neat, cool, spacious, and fragrant with flowers," as one visitor recorded. The house was the perfect setting for this gentle soft-spoken woman who devoted herself to her husband and children. Between 1840 and 1855 the family lived in a dwelling on Pleasant Street in Amherst, but in October of 1855 moved back to the family homestead on Main Street. Mrs. Dickinson suffered a stroke in 1875—her world having fallen apart with the death of her husband the previous year—and was a partial invalid until her death in 1882. She was nursed with fidelity during those years by her daughter, Emily.

WILLIAM AUSTIN DICKINSON 1829-1895

Austin, the first child of the marriage of Edward and Emily Dickinson, was born on April 16, 1829. He taught school in Boston (1851-52), went on to study law at Harvard, and practiced in Amherst, where he spent the rest of his life. After his marriage to Susan Gilbert in Geneva, New York, on July 1, 1856, he settled with his bride in a newly-built home next to the family homestead on Main Street. Three children were born: Ned, Martha and Thomas.

Austin's father, at one point, compared the letters his son wrote from Harvard to the writing of Shakespeare and contemplated publishing them because of their literary merit. There is no existing description of family approval being accorded to the writing of Emily Dickinson; indeed, she concealed the main body of her work from her family and appears to have shown them only her light and occasional poems. Austin died in 1895; Susan, in 1913.

EMILY ELIZABETH DICKINSON 1830-1886

Emily was born on December 10, 1830. As a child she was much in awe of her father, but was devoted throughout her life to both her parents. She attended Amherst Academy for seven years, graduating in 1847, and spent one year at Mount Holyoke Female Seminary in South Hadley, Massachusetts. In the years following 1848, she settled down to the customary life of a New England village. She had been the wit of her class and well liked. A school friend remembers her as "not beautiful, yet she had great beauties. Her eyes were lovely auburn, soft and warm, her hair lay in rings of the same colour all over her head, and her skin and teeth were fine." One who met her in later life found her "a plain, shy little person, the face without a single good feature, but with eyes, as she herself said, "like the sherry the guest leaves in the glass," and with smooth bands of reddish chestnut hair. She had a quaint and nunlike look, as if she might be a German canoness of some religious order..." and she spoke "under her breath, in childlike fashion." There was, he said, "no trace of affectation" in her manner, and he confessed that he found her a total "enigma."

Her life was uneventful—visits to Boston, Cambridge and Worcester in 1844; a visit with relatives in Boston in 1845 and 1851; a brief stay in Washington and Philadelphia in 1854; and,

in 1864, visits to Boston for medical treatment for her eyes. In contrast to the placid exterior existence she led stand her poems which reflect an inner world of tumult, exaltation and intense creativity. In June 1884 she suffered a nervous collapse—death, she said, had wronged her by its too frequent visitations.

Even as a child Emily Dickinson felt estranged from religion as she saw it expressed and experienced around her. In the spring of 1846, when a religious revival swept through Amherst, she remarked, "the small circle who met for prayer missed me from their number." She was then fifteen. She gave vent to her little heresies in letters to friends throughout her life, remarking on one occasion, "I wish the 'faith of the fathers' didn't wear brogans and carry blue umbrellas," and frequently indulging in open scorn of cherished doctrines.

In her mid-twenties Emily Dickinson rebelled against the orthodoxy of her church, and although she would sometimes attend meetings, she withdrew membership to pursue her spiritual life on her own terms. It is thought that the tightly-structured metres and stanzas she used in her verse were influenced by the quatrains of the hymnal with which she was familiar. The themes of both her poems and her letters are, as her critics have pointed out, those ancient ones of which significant poetry is fashioned: the ecstasy of faith, the doubts which assail one who would believe, the struggle of the soul to understand its pain and growth, death, the anguish of parting, the lure of eternity. Her soul was all things to her— inspirator, friend, counsellor, elusive lover and the essential focus of her attention. She is, *par excellence,* the poet of the inner country, the landscape of the soul, the central tension governing her work being "the light of reunion and the fire of separation."[1] Her letters, no less than her poems, place her in the tradition of self-awareness, and reveal that their author is inescapably and instinctively a poet: scattered among descriptions of the weather, scraps of village gossip and reports of the small events which comprised her day are phrases and aphorisms which leap toward one claiming attention. "My business is circumference," she might suddenly remark in an otherwise pedestrian passage.

---

1 Bahá'u'lláh, *Tablet of Maqsúd*

Increasingly, Emily Dickinson withdrew from village activities, gradually ceased to leave home at all, and eventually became virtually a recluse in her father's house. Until her death on May 15, 1886, of a condition diagnosed as Bright's disease she did, however, remain solicitous of village life and maintained contact, in person and through correspondence, with a wide circle of friends and acquaintances. During the last years of her life she was, to many in the village, only that dim figure they glimpsed flitting about the garden, clad always in white; she was thought to have been thwarted in love, or mad. Here was the seed that later bloomed into the romantic legend of Emily Dickinson, one which for so long a period threatened to overshadow her achievement as a great poet and delay her deserved recognition. Her output was extraordinary. Although only seven of her poems were published in her lifetime—some anonymously and edited without consent—a total of 1,775 were discovered in a bureau drawer after her death. Her posthumous fame began with the gradual publication of her poems in editions between 1890 and 1955. Her manuscripts were purchased in 1950 by Gilbert H. Montague who presented them to the Harvard College Library. A workable edition of her output became available when Thomas H. Johnson published her poems in three volumes (1955) and her letters in three volumes (1958) for Harvard University. These publications made possible more serious study of her accomplishment but have done little to enable critics to solve the enigma of Miss Dickinson or penetrate her inviolable privacy. Serious students and admirers of Emily Dickinson should avail themselves of the opportunity of reading George Frisbie Whicher's *This Was a Poet* (1938); the Harvard edition of the *Poems*, edited by T. H. Johnson (1955); the Harvard edition of the *Letters*, edited by T. H. Johnson and Mrs. Theodora Ward (1958); Jay Leyda's helpful *The Years and Hours of Emily Dickinson* (Archon ed. 1970); and Richard B. Sewall's superlative *The Life of Emily Dickinson* (1974, 1980). Inder Nath Kher's insightful *The Landscape of Absence* (1974) sheds light on the poems. A new wave of scholarly work is in preparation or has just been released. Emily Dickinson is, in Mr. Sewall's telling tribute, "inexhaustible." Some scholars are convinced that Emily was aware of her own genius and arranged her life to meet its demands.

LAVINIA DICKINSON 1833-1899

Emily's sister was born on February 28, 1833, the "baby of the family." The girls were close friends all their lives, but Lavinia did not enjoy Emily's full confidence, as evidenced by her astonishment in coming across a cache of Emily's poems after her sister's death. Her range of interests, as reflected in Emily's letters, seems to have been confined (in Emily's comment) to her "pussies and posies," though brother Austin remarked that she could "raise an *awful* breeze"—a reference to her sharp tongue and peppery spirit. Like Emily, "Vinnie" or "Vinnia" did not marry, and she remained in her father's home until her death in 1899. After Emily's death, and by her sister's direction, Lavinia destroyed all of the correspondence received by Emily. Had it survived many of the questions which now tantalize scholars might have found answers.

MARGARET MAHER - "MAGGIE"

Margaret "Maggie" Maher was born in Parish Kilusty in Tipperary and came to the United States in that flood of immigrants who entered in the latter half of the nineteenth century. She was over twenty when she came into the service of the Dickinson family in March 1869 and remained until the end, becoming the pivot and mainstay of the household. Her correspondence with a former employer, Clarinda Boltwood, miraculously survived and both her letters and those of Emily Dickinson indicate that friendship and respect flowered between the two women. Emily tirelessly sang her praises in her letters to friends, describing her as the "North Wind of the family—warm and wild and mighty." She became a buffer between Emily and the world, being called upon to slip letters clandestinely under Emily's door in periods of seclusion, and to rid the house of unexpected callers by presenting them with Miss Emily's excuses and gifts of flowers.

THOMAS WENTWORTH HIGGINSON

When Emily Dickinson's poems first attracted attention and enthusiastic admiration, Thomas Wentworth Higginson (1823-1911) was assigned the role of the villain of the piece, it being charged that in introducing her work to the public he doctored and mutilated it in order to win acceptance for it among a public with a taste for valentine verse. Later study, it has been suggested, indicates that he performed a useful service in hastening her acceptance and recognition and that his editing facilitated an understanding of her work. In any event, he was a kind, intelligent and honorable man whose motives were above reproach. The author in the present work has a little fun at Higginson's expense but pleads poetic license in using him as a symbol of all that is gray, stiflingly ordinary and disastrously well-intentioned—the very epitome of conventions which Emily Dickinson was striking out against in her poems and her interior life. One remembers her scorn of "dimity convictions!" Her private view of Higginson she discreetly left unexpressed.

Higginson was a Unitarian clergyman, the colonel of a Negro regiment in the Civil War, and an editor and critic with the *Atlantic Monthly*. He represented the standards of genteel literary taste which then prevailed. He was one of the few persons outside the family—the writer Helen Hunt Jackson was another—to whom Emily showed her work, but even her family had no idea of its volume. She wrote to him in 1862 asking if he thought her verse was "alive." This was her attempt to reach out to the world for editorial opinion. She drew her conclusions from his reply and although she maintained correspondence with Higginson for a number of years and continued to show him poems, now and again, the urgency was gone: she recognized that the literary world he represented was closed to her.

Higginson found her quaint, enigmatic and startling, but developed an affection for his erratic correspondent and recognized immediately that her gift was unique. He visited her in 1870 and again in 1873, and after her death published an account of his visit in the *Atlantic*. The preference of that time was for decorous, bland, moralizing, exhortatory poetry, and although Higginson recognized her native genius, it was beyond his range of appreciation. He was much troubled by her crudity of diction, disquieted by her subject matter and alarmed by her "fractures of grammar and dictionary." She remained an enigma to him from beginning to end. His account of his first visit with her is very valuable, and reveals the chasm between the arbiter of literary fashion and the Amherst poet: they lived in different worlds. Her "immortal wine," it might be said, was too heady for the parson accustomed to cambric tea.

EMILY'S SUITORS

THE LAW STUDENT

Benjamin Franklin Newton was a young law student who worked for a time (1847 to 1849) in her father's law office. He shared books and thoughts with Emily Dickinson and became (in Emily's words) her "gentle, grave Preceptor" possessing "an intellect far surpassing [her] own" and thought of as a dearly-loved "elder brother." He left Amherst to set up his own practice and not long afterwards died of tuberculosis. He is thought to be the one Emily described in a letter to Higginson as the friend who "ventured too near immortality and never returned." A romance might be inferred, but this is generally considered to be inconclusive.

THE REV. CHARLES WADSWORTH

Emily Dickinson met the Rev. Charles Wadsworth when she was twenty-five, during a visit to Washington where her father was serving as a Congressman. Wadsworth was in his late forties— successful, attractive, a minister of religion. It is possible to consider him as the major figure in her emotional life, the man to whom she gave her heart fully. It is thought that Wadsworth is the one referred to when Emily described to Higginson a friend "who was not content that I be his scholar—so he left the land." Some commentators suggest that the Rev. Wadsworth was the element in Emily Dickinson's life which triggered her great creative outburst during the 1860's; in 1862 alone she wrote 356 poems.

JUDGE OTIS P. LORD

After 1862, Judge Otis P. Lord of Salem, a widower in his late sixties and an old friend of the Dickinson family, often visited Amherst. Drafts of fifteen of Emily's letters written between 1878 and 1883 have given rise to the not unfounded speculation that she conceived strong feelings of love for him and perhaps even desired marriage.

SOME CORRESPONDENTS

Samuel and Mary Bowles: Old and valued family friends. Bowles edited the Springfield *Republican.*

Joseph K. Chickering: A teacher of English at Amherst College.

James D. Clark: On Wadsworth's death in 1882, Emily Dickinson exchanged with his friend, James Clark, memories of their mutual friend, and later with his brother, Charles Clark.

Perez Dickinson Cowan: A school friend of Emily's at Amherst College who entered the ministry.

Josiah and Elizabeth Holland: Dr. and Mrs. J. G. Holland were among Emily's closest friends. Dr. Holland was on the staff of the Springfield *Republican* and went on to become editor of *Scribner's Monthly.*

Louise and Fannie Norcross: Cousins of Emily Dickinson with whom she maintained close bonds all her life.

Abiah Root: A school friend of Emily's with whom she corresponded frequently until Abiah's marriage.

Mrs. Edward Tuckerman: Wife of the professor of botany at Amherst College.

Kate Turner: A friend with whom she corresponded between 1859 and 1866.

Maria Whitney: A Dickinson family friend who lived at Northampton.

Abby Wood: A school friend who married a missionary, the Reverend Daniel Bliss, with whom she went to Beirut and there helped him found the Syrian Protestant College (later known as the American University of Beirut) which was attended by Shoghi Effendi, Guardian of the Bahá'í Faith. Elsewhere I have drawn attention to the fact that Emily Dickinson was a contemporary of the heroic Ṭáhirih (1817-1852), Persian poet and martyr. For those who muse over patterns it should be recorded here that Mount Holyoke, attended by Emily, was the recipient of a Tablet from 'Abdu'l-Bahá, dated July 24, 1919. See *United States Bahá'í News,* September 1973, p. 19.

What shall we do, my darling, when trial grows more and more,
when the dim, lone light expires, and it's dark, so very
dark, and we wander, and know not where, and cannot get
out of the forest — whose is the hand to help us, and to
lead, and forever guide us; they talk of a "Jesus of
Nazareth" — will you tell me if it be he?

Emily Dickinson

PART ONE:

SPRING SONG 1841-1859

*O Children of Negligence! Set not your
affections on mortal sovereignty and
rejoice not therein. Ye are even as
the unwary bird that with full
confidence warbleth upon the bough;
till of a sudden the fowler Death
throws it upon the dust, and the
melody, the form and the colour are
gone, leaving not a trace. Wherefore
take heed, O bondslaves of desire!*

Bahá'u'lláh

SPRING SONG

My hope put out white petals
In tentative delight
But twice there came concussive frost,
Obliterating blight

Which, blotting out my April,
Stirred wisdom in my root.
Should another burgeoning come
Will twig renew? 'Tis moot.

CHANT

I chant the words that comfort me —
Bird and *peach* and *hills* and *tree* —
And skimming through the garden chime
Sounds and syllables I'd make mine.
Some words bubble on my lips —
Gentian, damson, water, ships —
And some from deeper source are sprung
Whose taste is holy on my tongue,
Words that tell the all of me —
Flight and *immortality* —
Countering those which catch the breath:
Shadow, darkness, ice and *death.*

MAY ONE WALTZ?

Amherst College
May 7, 1845

Dear Abiah,

How large they sound, the studies here,
Botany and Latin!
Need one be prim to study them?
May one still waltz in satin?

Have you a herbarium
As most the girls here do?
Are you, like me, acclaimed school wit? —
A station one might rue!

The belle of Amherst I shall be
When I am seventeen —
Disdainful of admirers,
A veritable queen!

When next we meet I hope you'll find
Your Emily somewhat wiser;
If not, I trust you'll have the sense
Politely to advise her.

A letter would be welcome, dear,
And, oh! before I end —
Enclosed is a geranium leaf,
Please press it for your friend,

Emily
(age 14)

BREAD

Mother thinks me not able to confine myself to school this term. She had rather I would exercise, and I can assure you I get plenty of that article by staying at home. I am going to learn to make bread tomorrow. So you may imagine me with my sleeves rolled up, mixing flour, milk, saleratus, etc., with a deal of grace . . .

Emily Dickinson

. . . her father demanded that she be the sole author of all his bread . . .

Jay Leyda

Amherst, 1845

Dear Abiah,

My brow is moist, I bite my lips,
I flaunt domestic scars;
A badge of flour decks my cheek
As Meg's or Kate's, and mars

My fourteen years of dignity
As tranquilly I reigned,
A secluded parlour scholar
Who drudgery disdained.

A kitchen hour swept away
My carefree sovereignty;
And where's the yeast to puff again
My former majesty?

What kneading will our lives sustain —
What flame or blaze embrace
Till judge awards approving smile
As now lights mother's face?

But oh! the crust is tawny
And proudly I admire;
Were resurrection so assured
Who'd fail to brave the fire?

Your Affectionate Emily

THE PRISONER

... many an hour has fled with its report to heaven, and what has been the tale of me?

Emily Dickinson

... if the anguish of others helped one with one's own, now would be many medicines.

Emily Dickinson

I am in bondage to my bones!
My spirit raised a shout,
But all negotiation failed
To bring the captive out.

No resolution yet is found
Despite the urgent cry.
Release me! pleads the prisoner;
Say bones: *But then we die!*

No cunning plan the spirit weaves —
Now pining, tortured, thin —
Overthrows bones' tyranny
By mutiny within.

A meteor's rash leap by night
Or azure glimpsed through bars
Encourages the sore inmate
To stride across the stars.

Long has the chafing struggle raged
And God alone can know
When might the captive, fervour gained,
Slip his lax chains and go.

HOME, SWEET HOME

When we contemplate Emily Dickinson, we cannot fail to be struck by the contrast between her calm, eventless outward existence, and the titanic struggles going on within.

John Wain

Dear Abiah ... We all went home on Wednesday before Thanksgiving. ... Never did Amherst look more lovely to me, and gratitude rose in my heart to God, for granting me such a safe return to my *own dear home* ... all were at the door to welcome the returned one. ... Oh, Abiah, it was the first meeting, as it had been the first separation, and it was a joyful one to all of us. ... Slowly and sadly dragged a few of the days after my return to the Seminary, and I was very homesick, but ... my sorrows were soon lost in study, and I again felt happy, if happiness there can be away from "home, sweet home."

Emily Dickinson

No insurrection mars the calm
In which we glide about
Like somnambulant leviathans
Whose temper none will doubt.

We serenely pass and circumvent,
A fixed course marked for each,
But I have dreamed an atmosphere
Beyond whale's ken or reach —

A stratosphere where leaping fish
Would parry, flash and dart
And spark from their vitality
The force that suns impart

And careening as hot meteors,
If writhing creatures met,
Collision strikes them into flame
For love could not be wet.

But docilely I loll in murk
Where minnow must remain
And if I called these waters love
I knew no other name.

24

VALENTINE

Every night have I looked, and yet in vain, for one of Cupid's messengers. Many of the girls have received very beautiful valentines; and I have not and had been hoping for one... I am pining for a valentine.

Emily Dickinson

Mount Holeyoke Female Seminary
South Hadley
February 1848

That I shall claim your face once more!
If heaven offered nothing more
Love's reverent labour I'd perfect
Till there its image I'd detect;
Witless, hapless, overjoyed,
Delighting I'd been so employed
In life's benevolent career
To seek and find and choose the dear —
Task unheard, unsung as flowers'
Yet highest use of earth's short hours —
Sweet choice by Providence afforded
Overflowingly rewarded;
All paradise profoundly awed
By visage only beauty flawed,
Angels in hushed consternation
Watching God smile approbation.
Till heaven's gained, I am content
To memorize emolument.

GRADUATION

[Emily Dickinson] is the poet of the inscrutable necessity which we endure. . . . In her best poems, those that deal directly and boldly with suffering and death, she is governed by the sublime.

Daniel G. Hoffman

Attentive is the scholar
That Master, pain, instructs;
A vivid erudition
His tutelage inducts.

The standard set on Calvary
Informs curriculum —
So imperial a knowledge
As strikes the pupil dumb.

Examination's agony
Brings student sharpest ruth
If sought promotion slips his grasp —
Attainment, Beauty, Truth.

PRAYER

Mother is still an invalid ... father and Austin still clamour for food; and I, like a martyr, am feeding them ... looking around my kitchen, and praying for kind deliverance. ... *My* kitchen, I think I said. God forbid that it was or should be my own—God keep me from what they call *households*, except that bright one of "faith!"

Emily Dickinson

Deliver me from cooking-stoves,
From kitchens, pots and pans;
The only menu I select
Is that which heaven plans.

Release me from the laundry tub,
The martyred clothes on line;
Let imperishable garment,
Unsoiled and white be mine.

I take no pride in baking bread,
The golden loaf a vision;
I ask higher resurrection,
The leavened soul risen.

Spare this maid assault of steam
Who pleads for distillation
And seeks for fruits she puts away
Eternal preservation.

Dash not the crockery of her hopes
But grant long use instead
Till night declares the final meal
And servant seeks her bed.

VETERAN

I struggled with temptation,
Denial was the cost.
Finally I conquered
Though heavy was my loss.

Not a glorious victory,
No sound of rolling drum
Nor young girls tossing flowers
To welcome victor home;

An almost inadvertent triumph
From which the heart recoils,
The limping soldier footsore,
Indifferent to the spoils;

Not hearing the faint music,
Unmindful of the flag,
Not one shout raised to cheer him,
No eye to brighten, glad;

Nor trophy to proclaim him
The hero who had won —
All his wounds invisible,
All his courage gone.

Across his soul's scarred battlefield
Where all his pride was slain
The legions of his enemy
Prepare to strike again.

THANKSGIVING
1851

We are thinking most of Thanksgiving than anything else just now—how full will be the circle, less than by none—how the things will smoke—how the board will groan with the thousand savory viands... Thanksgiving indeed to a family united once more together before they go away...

Emily Dickinson

Dear Austin,

Without you we are lacking jokes —
Sobriety's our way!
I'd gorge on laughter for a week
If you'd come home to stay.

We now put poetry aside
With laudable intention;
Father says life's very *real* and
Asks our strict attention.

Father's *real* and mine collide
(Unharmed, we've both escaped!)
But brushing his world in the dark
I feel my elbow's scraped.

At my request he buys me books
But begs me not to read them;
He fears they *joggle* the staid mind —
My heart persuades I need them.

Mother's health is better now
And sister Vinnie's fine;
Both join in my prayer that you'll
Not miss Thanksgiving time.

The apples are alerted, dear,
The grapes were spoken to
And all await royal visit of
Good son and brother—you!

Emily

SAWDUST

Dear Austin . . . If I hadn't been afraid that you'd "poke fun" at my feelings,
I had written a sincere letter, but since "the world is hollow, and dollie's
stuffed with sawdust," I really do not think we had better expose our
feelings . . .

Emily Dickinson

The next time you decline to write,
Do write and let me know;
The protraction of the insult
Is why I suffer so.

The next time you won't speak to me,
Do stop and tell me why;
The silence that is unexplained
Brings stinging tear to eye.

The next time I'm invisible,
Do try to catch my glance;
I'll don my best identity
And bid you ask me dance.

The next time I am orphaned,
Convey complaint to mother —
And if I've not mislaid my kin,
I'll claim you as my brother.

CONTEMPT

Speak of the moderns without contempt, and of the ancients without idolatry.

Phillip Dormer Stanhope (1694-1773)
Earl of Chesterfield

Dear Austin . . . Father was very severe to me . . . he gave me quite a trimming about "Uncle Tom" and "Charles Dickens" and those "modern literati" who, he says, are nothing, compared to past generations who flourished when he was a boy . . . so I'm in disgrace at present, but I think of that "pinnacle" on which you always mount when anybody insults you, and that's quite a comfort to me . . .

Emily Dickinson

A distance down — uncounted miles —
I hear a muffled sound
Of less concern to summit peaks
Than is a rabbit's bound.

My thoughts are those of eagles,
I know the hawk's sharp cry,
Aloof in pinnacled contempt
I snub the strident fly.

I do not hear the sea complain —
Companion of the cloud,
I seek entry to Olympus
Where gods and silence crowd

In agreeable assembly;
I plead in rapt content —
So voluble my quietude
All give tongue-tied assent.

ABRAHAM AND THE NIGHTINGALE

...how we all loved Jenny Lind ["The Swedish Nightingale"], but not accustomed oft to her manner of singing didn't fancy *that* so well as we did *her.* No doubt it was very fine, but take some notes for her *Echo,* the bird sounds from the *Bird Song,* and some of her curious thrills, and I'd rather have a Yankee. Father sat all evening looking *mad* ... as if old Abraham had come to see the show, and thought it was all very well, but a little excess of *monkey!* She took $4000 for tickets at Northampton aside from all expenses...

Emily Dickinson

Amherst
July 5, 1851

Dear Austin,

I took a carriage through the rain
To hear the songbird tweet;
I'll never do the same again —
A foreign and costly treat.

The acrobatic curlicues!
The vocal hanky-panky!
I'd ask less fanfare and to-do —
I'd rather have a Yankee!

Such goings-on are very well
But life's an earnest bind;
There's Satan, Hell and Judgment Day
To occupy the mind.

A hint of exile in her eyes,
A sadness in the voice,
To contradict the lilting tone
That bade the heart rejoice.

Transporting to another world!
Urging us to follow!
I've no taste for frivolity;
Monkey-shines are hollow.

The way the song enveloped us —
Invisible, its snare!
The challenge of its soft address:
Follow, if you dare!

Who cares a fig for Nightingales,
The cadence palls but soon;
A hooting train, a chickadee —
Now *there's* a Yankee's tune!

Emily

THE TRAVELER

(After a celebration of the opening of a railroad to New London, 1853)

Dear Austin... The New London day passed off grandly, so all the people said. It was pretty hot and dusty, but nobody cared for that. Father was, as usual, chief marshal of the day, and went marching around with New London at his heels like some old Roman general upon a trimph day.... I sat in Professor Tyler's woods and saw the train move off, and then came home again for fear somebody would see me, or ask how I did...

Emily Dickinson

A loud *hurrah!* ignites the town,
The strong cheer catches fire,
The hills awaken grumbling
That solitude expires.

Flags adorn the rostrum where
Officials swell with pride;
The village struts excitedly
To see the dream made live.

I-told-you-so! runs through the streets
Electric as a shiver;
The noisy cry of celebrants —
We did it! — rings the river.

A pulsating locomotion
To transport all away;
One — silent in the smoke and din —
Much traveled, who will stay.

The brief jaunt to New London starts,
There boards a jostling throng.
But one seeks New Jerusalem
And knows her journey long.

THREE WORDS

Had I — was there — a summer?
I see the fields have gone,
The vagrant population
All fled or gathered — gone.

As though a floor had emptied —
Dancer, cadence, sped.
I'm left without an emblem
Except three words you said.

Life is short, you told me,
And then I lost your glance.
Such a searing education
An April hour grants!

HOPE

The hangnail of small circumstance
Will cause our hopes to snag —
The letter lost, the tryst not kept,
Then droops the tattered flag.

At littlest sign — a crocus —
Our expectations flow.
Knew we how deep the token lay
We would not let her go.

ONE

One is such a dainty sum —
One bird, one cage, one flight;
One note to sound in unseen wood
Perhaps for God's delight.

A legion would be comfort,
A multitude were bliss;
A frugal hand assigned but one
And calls back even this.

LADIES' VERSE

Emily Dickinson seems often to be caught by conventions of prosody or to have relaxed into them, and often she seems merely to echo thoughts that reflect the safe, worn attitudes to Nature, Society or Human Woe that were the nineteenth century's particular poetic counters. Even her admirers must admit that much of her work is almost indistinguishable from the "ladies' verse" that cluttered the journals of her time. Perhaps no other major poet in America or elsewhere has written so many reams of maudlin bad verse.

John Malcolm Brinnin

Only those who are capable of writing well can write really badly.

David Wright

I

Who will mind the fitting
Who knows she'll have a gown?
The patience and the pinning
Improve the frock she'll own.

Who will mind the heavy cross
Who knows she'll have a crown?
The bearing and the struggling
Reward with richer one.

Who will mind the dying
Who knows she'll have a life?
Life is death we're lengthy at —
The dying gives relief.

II

Much bouquet on the window pane,
A trace of moss and fern
Painted by ethereal hand
Whose art no pupils learn.

A nosegay for an angel,
Gathered, etched by night,
To ease rainbow-besotted eye —
Its only palette white.

III

... the least memorable of the several Emily Dickinsons ... is the coy Emily
who ... flirts with all the creatures of the earth and air as if she were the
inhabitant of a nineteenth-century Disneyland.

John Malcolm Brinnin

I have befriended little things
And shared their guileless pleasure,
Have interviewed unguardedly
Small colonies at leisure.

I've chatted with the Cockney bees,
With orioles and jays;
Melodic frogs have sung to me,
I know the cricket's ways.

The universe so overwhelms
With brash giants overgrown,
The small consort with small to shrink
A world too vast to own.

THE SERMON

When she was twenty-four, [Emily Dickinson] refused to become a member of the church, though she still attended services sporadically. It was a major decision for her, and an expression of her integrity and strong will. She distrusted the lasting value of emotional conversion. Freedom of spirit was of paramount importance to her.

Peter Jones

The chief tension in her work comes from... her inability to accept the orthodox religious faith of her day and her longing for the spiritual comfort of it...

The New Columbia Encyclopedia

The minister today... preached about death and judgment, and what would become of those, meaning Austin and me, who behaved improperly — and somehow the sermon scared me.... He preached such an awful sermon... that I didn't think I should ever see you again until Judgment Day, and then you wouldn't speak to me, according to his story. The subject of perdition seemed to please him, somehow. It seems very solemn to me...

Emily Dickinson

I beg you, learned sir, to tell
Who here is saint, who infidel?
Though I would seek infinity
I bow to your authority
And know your eye is trained to see
Such sins as are concealed in me
Admiring your cheerful tone
When driving the grim message home.
Where is gained the erudition
To speak, at first hand, of perdition?
A gloomy subject I had thought —
My childish whimsy like as not!
Though I might beg before I go
To know why you revere it so?

38

Most impressive was your relish
When depicting matters hellish —
Do, pray, forgive that naughty word,
I'm just a woman, thus absurd.
Perchance you saw the bonnets shake
Throughout the church for virtue's sake
And our dainty consternation
At your brimstone titillation.
No doubt in scripture you're well versed
But have you hell and heaven reversed?
I seek the way to heaven's gate
Which you obstruct, so I shan't wait;
I'll smile in hollow courtesy
And seek, alone, divinity.

BEYOND THE FOLD

Religion may be defined as what the individual does with his solitariness.

A. N. Whitehead

A citizen among her townsmen yet not subject to the rules by which they lived, she became a sort of hovering presence, the ornamental eccentric of a community independent enough to harbour her with as much pride as embarrassment.... Technically her [poetic] range is modest, based on the hymn meters she knew from church and school.... Her intelligence was double-edged, too sharp to accept the religion of her generation without making the private rejections orthodoxy would not countenance and altogether too great to be confined within the limits of the fastidious, genteel education to which proper young women of her day were subjected.... [One aspect] of Emily Dickinson's character is the saucy little rebel in God's back yard who teases words into the shapes of rococo valentines... who makes God "a noted clergyman"...

John Malcolm Brinnin

I heard the bell, saw gathered flock,
I knew the fold was warm,
And saw one creature obdurate
Yet felt but mild alarm.

I knew him fed, I knew him free,
I knew his absence mourned,
But thought that should the wolf affright
His cry the flock had warned.

And should he fall beneath the fang
It gives no cause to weep
That greater pen enfold the lamb
In everlasting keep.

Then ring the bell and call the flock,
Ingather all that stray,
But mark the beast intractable
The fields invite to stay.

EMILY'S SONG

When she writes her address, she puts down Main Street, Amherst,
Massachusetts, but she means The Mind of God.

John Malcolm Brinnin

Had hearts the art of porcelain
The mending were small feat
But I have owned one whose repair
Earth's craftsmen can't complete.

Had love asked only giving
The donor were content
But I have known a stealthy hand
Twice prove our loves are lent.

Had death comprised mere dying
The handiwork were sweet
But I mark its keen audition
In every eye I greet.

Had minds a spacious attic
The past were soon antique
But I have one too visited
Where grief renews to speak.

Had heaven held sure solace
To hasten there were wise
But I, grown timid, cautious,
Search for ambush, man's and sky's.

One day I'll meet fate's boldest stare
And ask its harsh command
My apron full of gentian and
Lone daisy in my hand.

Till then, like Jonah in the dark,
I ride the journey out
And count truth's ribs, bemused that faith
So multiplies my doubt.

41

THE OLD SUITOR

Pardon my sanity, Mrs. Holland, in a world *in*sane, and love me if you will, for I had rather *be* loved than to be called a king in earth, or a lord in Heaven.

Emily Dickinson

... romantic renunciation humanized the austerity of the record; and a doughty spirit asserting itself over religion and society alike made her story heroic.

John Malcolm Brinnin

I put my little life away,
Arranged it in a chest;
Brushed carefully and smoothed its folds —
I would not have it crease

Nor fade or stain or be too worn
When taken up again.
"I'll wear it when I'm loved," said I,
But waited long in vain.

I came upon it just today,
The fashion seeming odd,
But slipped it on to pirouette
And please my glass and God.

MOVING HOUSE

I cannot tell you how we moved. I had rather not remember... I took at the time a memorandum of my several senses, and also of my hat and coat, and my best shoes—but it was lost in the mêlée, and I am out with lanterns, looking for myself... the pantomime contained in the word "moved"... is a kind of *gone-to-Kansas* feeling.

Emily Dickinson

It's a *gone-to-Kansas* feeling,
The moving of one's house.
One's effects packed in a handbox,
One leaves behind the mouse,

The long-endured familiar draughts,
A faithful flowering tree —
At the window, as we pull away,
Distraught, a former me

Signals that I leave behind
Uninventoried days,
But the wagon moves despite my cry,
Its progress none delays.

I cross what seem like deserts,
An aeon on the road;
The pinched face at the window,
The frantic hand that showed

Tell of the irretrievable,
Volubly as tombs —
That creature in the wainscot!
The echoes in the rooms!

FOREVER, NOW

... wicked as I am, I read my Bible sometimes ... I'm half tempted to take my seat in that Paradise of which the good man writes, and begin forever and ever *now*, so wondrous does it seem.

Emily Dickinson

All the good by summer given
I take upon my tongue
And break the flesh to drink the juice;
The taste is never done.

All the good the sun has coaxed
I bracket with my eye;
And though the doll close her wax lid
The image does not die.

THE DEMOCRAT

I cannot stay any longer in a world of death. Austin is ill of fever. I buried
my garden last week — our man, Dick, lost a little girl through the scarlet
fever.... Ah! democratic Death! Grasping the proudest zinnia from my
purple garden, — then deep to his bosom calling the serf's child!

Emily Dickinson

He plucks the proudest zinnia
I'd prized but never held
Then turns his eye upon a child
As casually felled.

Each kingdom that attracts his glance
Seized callously upon —
Insect, robin, pippin —
All realms to him are one.

The tallest towers a city boasts,
Warrior's broad brave breast,
The shrinking girl — he covets all,
Dread, democratic Death,

To crowd his dwelling on cold slopes
Where lovers sleep alone;
Heaven's selective tyranny
Affords a kinder home —

A bosom's feathered comfort —
Death clasps to iced, mean bone;
Heaven pillows with fulfilment,
Death with unyielding stone.

He stalks across my choicest day
To plunder all I see.
I challenge, hand upraised in faith,
His dark democracy.

PROMENADE

... during her seventeenth year, while at Mount Holyoke, the evangelical movement reached the village and seminary. Many of her fellow students committed themselves ... Emily held back, even when her family gave way to the fervour of the movement.

Peter Jones

... she did not, and could not, accept the Puritan God at all. She was frankly irreverent, on occasion, a fact which seems to have made her editors a little uneasy.... What she was irreverent to, of course, was the Puritan conception of God, the Puritan attitude towards Him, [God being] in her day, a portentous Victorian gentleman.

Conrad Aiken

Matters of Calvinist sermons that her townsmen might mull over on their way home from church ... became part of the philosophic reaches of her solitary communion.

John Malcolm Brinnin

Our pastor says we are a "worm." How is that reconciled? ... Do you think we shall "see God?" Think of Abraham strolling with Him in genial promenade!

Emily Dickinson

When Abraham strolls out with God
In genial promenade,
The seraphs vie for vantage points
To watch the quaint parade

And glimpse the stalwart patriarch,
Prolific sire "of many,"
A wonder to all angelhood
(It's said they've not sired any.)

His march to Canaan they salute,
His attitude towards Lot,
His willingness to share his son —
(He loves each one begot.)

They cheer him for his Covenant,
Applaud his fertile feat —
But I would beg his "bosom"
And there locate my seat.

A MODEST GLASS

I might tug for a life and never accomplish it, but no one can stop our
looking on . . .

Emily Dickinson

When I turned back and closed my will
I heard a sparrow on the sill
So then took up my modest glass
And looked at him and looked at grass;

Saw tossing maples blithely red,
The dark wood where no word is said,
A girl who swirled in flashing gown
To have the music ease her frown.

I saw the church beside which sleep
Those whose legends headstones keep
And saw a gaunt guest lurk alone
To follow every mourner home.

Then overhead the sun went out.
I saw a man abort his shout.
One cupped his hands and drank his tears;
A third in darkness slew his fears.

Then robust dawn came striding in
As though the night had never been.
The village rose to bake its bread;
Too much was spoken, little said.

A silence seals my bolted will,
The small bird trembles on my sill.
Village, maples, hills will pass.
The sparrow, too. But not the glass.

PROMISSORY NOTE

As a young woman [Emily Dickinson], so Mrs. [Martha Dickinson] Bianchi, a niece, informed us in the preface to *The Single Hound* (1914), had several "love affairs," but there is no evidence that any of them was serious, and we have no right, without other testimony, to assume here any ground for the singular psychological change that came over her... if we seek for the causes of the psychic injury which so sharply turned her in upon herself, we can only speculate. Her letters, in this regard, give little light, only showing us again and again that the injury was deep.

Conrad Aiken

[One persona] of Emily Dickinson is the reclusive bride of silence—the radiant girl in white who tarries in the world like an ethereal visitor...

John Malcolm Brinnin

> I could not take you to my bed
> As lovers have in books I've read
> To place your head upon my breast
> In soft communion there caressed.
> I could not offer you my kiss
> Though earth might yield no fruit like this,
> Nor give my hand for you to grasp,
> Nor could your own my hair unclasp
> That it be our sole robe and sheet
> In that warm naked place we meet.
> My shrine's expectant perfumed air
> Heard not your footfall nor your prayer,
> Nor was the moment given me
> To learn your supple mystery
> And in that solitude to raise
> A grateful anthem in your praise.
> Your laden arms that held all good
> I could not reach for, though I would.
> Not mine to voice, the circumstance,
> That spun me gasping from your glance.
> But life I charge to pay its debt
> That all I am be made yours yet.
> I pledge, should Promissor but smile,
> To lay with you an endless while.

And he took unto him all these,
and divided them in the midst,
and laid each piece one against
another: but the birds divided
he not.

Genesis 15:10

Life is death we're lengthy at; death the
hinge to life...

Emily Dickinson

PART TWO:

SUMMER SONG 1860-1869

O Man of Two Visions! Close one eye
and open the other. Close one to the
world and all that is therein, and
open the other to the hallowed
beauty of the beloved.

Bahá'u'lláh

SUMMER SONG

No pebble mars the brook today,
No film subtracts from noon
And should I faint in daylight
My pillow would be June.

My skin receives the evening,
My eye owns all it scans
And should I faint beneath the moon
She'll reach out long white hands.

THE CALLER

We are all human, Mary, until we are divine, and to some of us, that is
far off, and to some as near as the lady ringing at the door; perhaps
that's what alarms.

Emily Dickinson

The lady's tread upon the step,
Her hand upon the bell,
And all the rattling house grows wise
As when a solemn knell

Will slash across our dailiness
And strangeness burns the throat —
Upon the choking question *Who?*
Our very hand will float

Pathetically, an abstract stalk —
Our ownership a day —
Reminding it is friable.
She does not turn away —

My heart knifed by insistent ring
I steel myself to go
With dread-swamped pulse to swing the door
Upon her fraught *hello.*

50

THE CRIMINAL

It is a criminal thing to be a boy in a godly village,
but maybe he will be forgiven.

Emily Dickinson

It is criminal to be a boy
(The village won't approve!)
The accomplice of disruptive joy
And unselective love.

Boys leap, or dawdle, dreaming,
A whistle on their lips,
Tell of distant dazzling worlds,
Lost treasure and foreign ships.

Boys rustle so with secrets —
We wince and look askance;
They're intimates of eagles' nests
And may, unbidden, dance.

Small fervours bulge their pockets,
Their grace is all awry,
They blurt of fabled things and sob
Because the phoenix dies.

They are fugitives from duty,
Shun our harsh pieties
Yet without pageantry they serve
No less our deity.

The fox knows their sly longing,
The trees have heard them pray;
I've known one store his lawless hopes
Where nothing may decay.

Bareheaded all the summer long
The boy, pell-mell, will pass,
Till criminal, betrayed like us,
Confess himself to grass.

DEVOTIONS

A mosquito buzzes round my faith
I think to name him doubt.
He's so persistent in his prayer
My own he quite drowns out.

But often, too, an oriole
In close eave-hugging vine
Shares my small mass — his matins
Not so rapt nor loud as mine.

DANCING

You speak of "disillusion." That is one of the few subjects on which
I am an infidel. Life is so strong a vision, not one of it shall fail.

Emily Dickinson

I miss the grasshoppers much, but suppose it is all for the best. I
should become too much attached to a trotting world.

Emily Dickinson

Were only one life given me,
To while its length away
I might dance through the village,
Weary my heels a day.

Benevolence has twinned my birth;
With two to regulate
I closet one and pocket one
And, dancing, feel no weight.

Two were a generosity
Beyond my power to own.
Ample is my cardinal choice
To dance the village down.

52

COSTUME

...I should love to see you dearly, girls.... You seem to take a smiling view of my finery. If you knew how solemn it was to me, you might be induced to curtail your jests. My sphere is doubtless calicoes, nevertheless I thought it meet to sport a little wool. The mirth it has occasioned will deter me from further exhibitions!

Emily Dickinson

...a plain, shy little person, the face without a single good feature...

T. W. Higginson

My sphere is doubtless calicoes,
An unpretentious stuff;
On bonnet, cape and parasol
No mitigating ruff

Of lace or ribbon to proclaim
The barn hen aggrandized;
The dun wren won't vex a peacock
Of rainbowed goods comprised.

I twist my hair severe in bun,
Blank ornaments my face;
My costume plain and stiff conceals
Beneath, cascades of lace.

In unredeemed convention,
I stroll and smile, polite;
Unguessed — luxurious tumults
Ravish my glass at night.

Brocades and satins, rarest silks,
A Sultan's jewelled display;
An Orient in my auburn fall
Tomorrow laid away.

An exchequer of unminted gold,
Spiced perfumes beauties spill;
All folded in a laquered box
To lie unspent and still.

COWARD'S CHOICE

Odd, that I, who say "no" so much, cannot bear it from others. Odd that I, who run from so many, cannot brook that one turn from me.

Emily Dickinson

I would not have you see me weep
If you should go away,
Nor show you yet another tear
If you decide to stay.

I cheat decision by my silence
Which wraps me like a shawl;
Reproach me not for rash consent
Should silence become my all.

No ultimatums pass my lips,
I give demands no voice,
And should you flee or linger here
I take no blame for choice.

To weep's a coward's penalty
Whose choice is not to choose:
For what she'll gain if you depart,
For — staying — what she'll lose.

THE HUNTER

Heaven hunts about for those
Who'd seek its peace below
Then it snatches them away
Occasioning angels, so.

How shall powerless innocence
Repeal predation's law
And the velvet mouse not tremble
To gauge the eagle's claw?

VERDICT REQUESTED

- The First Letter -

... It was in a handwriting so peculiar that it seemed as if the writer might have taken her first lessons by studying the famous fossil bird-tracks in the museum.... The impression of a wholly new and original poetic genius was ... distinct on my mind ... and with it came the problem never yet solved, what place ought to be assigned in literature to what is so remarkable, yet so elusive of criticism.... It is hard to say what answer was made by me ... to this letter. It is probable that the adviser sought to gain a little time and find out with what strange creature he was dealing. I remember to have ventured on some criticism ... and on some questions, part of which she evaded ... with a naive skill such as the most experienced and worldly coquette might envy ...

T. W. Higginson

Amherst
April 15, 1862

Mr. Higginson,

Are you too deeply occupied
To say if my verse lives?
The mind crowds very near itself
The judgment that it gives

Is clouded by proximity,
And since I've none to ask
You'd earn my quickest gratitude
Did you accept the task.

If no breath propels my lines
And you dared tell me so
I would honour you more deeply,
So beg you let me know.

That you will not betray me, sir,
Is needless to remark,
Since honour is its own best pawn.
Till you judge — Yours, in the dark,

E.D.

55

EVASION

— The Second Letter -

Of punctuation there was little; she used chiefly dashes [and] followed the Old English and present German method of [capitalizing] every noun substantive... sometimes there would arrive an exquisite little detached strain [but] many of her fragments were less satisfying. She almost always grasped whatever she sought, but with some fracture of grammar and dictionary on the way. Often, too, she was obscure, and sometimes inscrutable...

Thomas Wentworth Higginson

[Higginson's] account of her poetry... indicates how right she was to follow the eccentric bent of her own genius. The alternative was trying to conform to the age's ideas of what a lady poet should be... and present uplifting sentiments in decorous language. [Higginson] primly improved to "weight" [her use of] the muscular colloquialism "heft" [in one of her tropes].

Daniel G. Hoffman

One has a good deal of sympathy for Higginson. He thought that Emily Dickinson's poems were not good enough to be printed in the *Atlantic Monthly*.... In putting her question to him [she] wanted to hear the voice of consensus, of "the world of letters." She heard it. And though she continued to correspond with Higginson... though their relationship is pleasant, no greater question hinges on his judgment. [Her] second letter which seems so artlessly confiding, in fact illustrates [her] inviolable privateness.

John Wain

... when [the volumes of her poems and letters edited for Harvard University (1955-58) by Thomas H. Johnson] finally appeared, it became clear that the earlier editors of Emily Dickinson had been widely maligned... as Emily Dickinson wrote them, they would have engaged the interest of the reading public to a far lesser degree than in the form in which they had been earlier presented.

John Malcolm Brinnin

Amherst
April 25, 1862

Dear Sir,

I'm honoured, Mr. Higginson,
To know you scanned my verse,
And found your surgery painless —
I feared it might be worse.

Your editorial fingers,
So delicate and deft,
Have spared the dainty reader
My aberrant use of "heft."

You arbitrate the fashion
Of good literature, I feel,
And safeguard the cloyed palate
Of the proper and genteel.

How admirably you cater to
Propriety and purity;
You mend my fractured grammar
And attend to my obscurity.

The subject, Immortality,
Is one I'm prone to mention;
Delete discreetly rather than
Defy polite convention.

You think my gait spasmodic, sir,
My punctuation quaint;
Your readers must be grateful that
You saved them from my taint.

Correction fosters progress so
How fortunate am I
To have you tabulate my faults —
I'd rather wince than die.

57

You ask about my sources of
Poetic inspiration;
I wish the answer simply were
Emersonian elation

But a terror came upon me —
I feign that I am brave
And so whistle like the schoolboy
Who'd pass at night a grave.

My parents who are religious
Address in prayer eclipse;
My creed brings me a Presence felt
Whose beauty seals my lips.

My mother does not care for thought,
My father mistrusts books.
Their wicked daughter fondles them
And — dare I say it? — looks.

For poetry I've Mr. Keats
And, too, the lovers, Browning —
I add in haste they're married, sir,
For fear I've set you frowning.

For prose I turn to Ruskin, sir,
And Browne and *Revelations*;
The former quite delight me but
The last-named aids salvation.

My companions, sir, are sundown
And the distant purple hills;
My music, the pond's carols and
Birds' virtuosic trills.

I've not read Mr. Whitman's book —
Disgraceful, I was told —
Would you print, were grammer sound,
A narrative so bold?

You ask me, sir, how old I am;
In truth I made no verse
But one or two till recently —
Is not my answer terse?

How shall I improve my work,
Or is that unconveyed —
Like melody or witchcraft,
By other means conveyed?

I've a brother and a sister
And both are dear to me.
My Carlo sees but does not tell —
Canine civility!

Is this, then, what you'd have me tell?
I'd not fatigue or grieve you;
And winking enigmatic eye,
I smile and wave and leave you.

Emily

SONG OF THE LEAF

My dying tutor told me that he would like to live till I had been a poet. . . .
And when, far afterward, a sudden light on orchards, or a new fashion in
the wind troubled my attention, I felt a palsy, here, the verses just relieve.

Emily Dickinson

I seize my courage as a crutch
When fear commands my door,
And hobble to the page for ease
As cowards have before.

A sudden light, an altered wind,
And palsy shakes the leaf.
How slight a palliative, lines,
For ravages of grief.

NORTH

[Emily Dickinson] is the one for whom the unknowable is as present
to her vision as the view from her window.

John Malcolm Brinnin

The sailor cannot see the North
But knows the needle can
And so I launch into the mist
With compass in my hand

And though I find an Orient
My voyage is not blessed
Until I reach more stringent port —
Northbound, my naked breast.

A TOAST

When I was a little girl, I had a friend who taught me Immortality; but venturing too near, himself, he never returned. Soon after my tutor died, and for several years my lexicon was my only companion. Then I found one more, but he was not contented I be his scholar, so he left the land.

Emily Dickinson

The friend who ventured too near immortality was a young law student who worked for a short time in her father's law office, leaving to set up his own practice and shortly afterwards dying of tuberculosis; Emily Dickinson had shared books and thoughts with him. The infinitely more important figure who "... left the land" was evidently the Rev. Charles Wadsworth, the man to whom she appears to have given her heart and given it once and for all ... no one has found a signed statement that Emily Dickinson loved Wadsworth. But the evidence can fairly be called conclusive.

John Wain

Could you believe me without? I had no portrait, now, but am small like the wren; and my hair is bold like the chestnut bur; and my eyes, like the sherry in the glass, that the guest leaves. Would this do just as well?

Emily Dickinson

My eyes are sherry in the glass
The draining robbed of glow;
The drop rebukes the lonely host
Who let the dear guest go.

Goblet empty as betrayal
Dismays the shivering hand;
My eyes were yours to celebrate
Had you not left the land.

Perhaps you will remember them
As when I was your host;
A kinder gleam illumined then —
Full glass, upraised in toast.

My eyes were yours, my chestnut hair,
All powers I command;
Had you not left the land, my love,
Had you not left the land.

FAME

If [Emily Dickinson] is not the greatest woman poet, it is difficult, beyond the ancient praise that seals Sappho in the classic pantheon, to say who is.

John Malcolm Brinnin

If fame belonged to me, I could not escape her; if she did not, the longest day would pass me on the chase, and the approbation of my dog would forsake me then. My barefoot rank is better.

Emily Dickinson

Emily Dickinson conceded the impossibility of finding readers from the beginning; of the 1750 poems known to have been written by the Amherst recluse, only seven appeared while she was alive, and most of these without her consent and with extreme editorial revision of her text...

Daniel G. Hoffman

I pour my tea in thinnest cup —
Weightless, almost, to lift up;
No pattern mars its purity,
White my cup and pale my tea.

I place my slice upon a plate
Virginal and out of date
And think how small is fare of birds
That yet fly south. But where nest words?

Let mine be that frugal feast
Becoming those who ask the least.
I note in winter, robin gone,
The robust memory keeps his song.

THE TESTED

It is difficult not to be fictitious in so fair a place, but tests' severe repairs are permitted all.

Emily Dickinson

The orchard much attended,
So mercilessly pruned,
Revives to bear a fuller crop
And so to law attuned

I lift my branch as suppliant,
In confidence that yield
Increases at the gardener's touch
And bounty be revealed.

THE WEATHER IN AMHERST

My life has been too simple and stern to embarrass any...

Emily Dickinson

It was love that made my bosom surge,
The same that caused it shrivel,
That swept such arctic through my brain
As sheared it cold and level;

Yet nudged a tropic in my veins,
A sirocco stirred in blood,
Too frail to overthrow the frost
For all the sun's strong good;

And drew me to the homey tomb
Past anguished gales of reason,
To spurn heart's fickle weather
For soul's iron changeless season.

My scant iced signature was silence
Who scarce tugged sleeve of fame.
Do lovers faltering in the snow
Lisp, numb of lip, my name?

THE ONLY GAZE

I fear we shall care very little for the technical resurrection, when to behold
the one face that to us comprised it is too much for us, and I dare not
think of the voraciousness of that only gaze and its only return.

Emily Dickinson

Not to see what we love is very terrible, and talking doesn't ease it,
and nothing does but just itself. The eyes and hair we chose are all
there, to us...I often wonder how the love of Christ is done when
that below holds so.

Emily Dickinson

I thought, my love, when you were gone
I'd find new loves to look upon
And, desperate, searched a long sore while;
One had your face but not your smile
And one, resemblance of your hand
But not its supple, light command;
Another's voice, facsimile,
But lacked your song's felicity;
One, skill to pantomime your glance
But heard no music, knew no dance.
Still I search and have no rest
Until my eyes your two arrest
And it is given me to stare
Though kingdoms dim and planets wear,
Though heaven pales into a blur,
Its lapse incapable to stir
Till, unrestrained, the famished look
On one whose précis told love's book.

THE HOUSEGUEST

Dear Cousins —

She moves in a smart atmosphere
Her breast armoured in lace;
At her approach the trees stood straight,
The pansies mocked her grace.

The damsel has a dainty air
And wears a narrow boot.
Her glance starched the geraniums
And turned to glass the fruit.

And should she think to leave next week —
(Before she combs the lawn!) —
No less than *"Bon voyage!"* I'd wish —
(Forgive me!) — wish her gone.

Emily

THE COVENANT

Every day life feels mightier, and what we have the power to be,
more stupendous.

Emily Dickinson

Life gives so strong a covenant
Who shall not sign in trust?
Its smallest clause empowered to
Bind atom — sun, or dust.

To all-compelling contract,
Though codicil be pain,
Adheres the constant signatory
Till only God remains.

All that fidelity attracts
A lenient bench reviews;
Sealed by the very hand of God
Exquisite bond renews.

TO TARGET DRAWN

Life is so fast it runs away
Despite our sweetest *whoa*!
The breathless rider's carried
Where the steed would have him go.

Death plods as if reluctantly
Nor bribery spurs his feet
But, unerring, tracks the narrow breast
Where he and other meet.

THE UNINVITED

To everything but anguish
The mind will soon adjust;
Uninvited, that marauder,
Invading, trails his dust

About the scrupulous household
The tidy mind maintains,
Sets soiling boots on ottoman,
Remotest chamber gains —

Wrenches down the damask curtains,
Breaks housewife's favourite bowl
And storms up faith's chaste stairway
To bed the balking soul.

THE SHIPWRECK

It is November. The noons are more laconic now...

Emily Dickinson

Religious themes constantly preoccupy her. "You mention Immortality!" she said in a letter. "That is the Flood subject!"

Peter Jones

The noons are more laconic now
And nights are swiftly born;
Unrecognized Gibraltar lights
Recast the village, foreign —

Till it recedes and strands me here
As shipwreck whose pale shout
Fog-deafened vessel could not catch
So moved from sight. Without,

A lonely, cold infinity;
Within, my small desk, bare —
And had I voice I yet would call
The ship that vanished — where?

Beyond my candle darkness churns
And taunts the lost one — then
Invading blackly snuffs my light
And inundates my pen.

THE WOLF

You mentioned spring's delaying — I blamed her for the opposite. I
would eat evanesence slowly.

Emily Dickinson

The ravenousness of fondness is best disclosed by children....Is there
not a sweet wolf in us that demands its food?

Emily Dickinson

John Cody sees in Dickinson the characteristics of the emotionally starved
child, and has found her oral imagery especially compelling...

Vivian R. Pollak

I

The furred thing rises from its lair
To stalk the transient and fair;
If captured in a springing pounce
The snack's devoured inch by ounce.
Beast sated then will stretch and sleep
Repast forgotten. I would keep
A subtler spoon within my grasp
And charm the dainty to my clasp —
My appetite to place in mind
The cherished tidbit, thus to find
It served on delft of memory
Long gazed upon adoringly.
Unnibbled, it will never fade
Nor will my slavering palate jade
Until a distant feast reveal
The morsel's my eternal meal.

II

If evanesence were the fare
How slowly I would dine,
And bibbed would circle round the board
To have it last a time.

Were immortality the dish
I'd leap across the floor
And seize it whole in both my hands
And beg the host for more.

DISCLOSURE

... I was thinking today, as I noticed, that the "Supernatural"
was only the Natural disclosed.

> Not "Revelation" 'tis that waits,
> But our unfurnished eyes.
>
> Emily Dickinson

The hieroglyphics gouged in air
By an impatient fire-gloved hand
Are given as our library —
We, star-affrighted, gaze to land

Where furnished in an atom's tome
Is erudition of the sky —
The dust-affronted student lifts
A blank uncomprehending eye

And swivelling will not read the book
From which his glance will dart again,
Though it's indexed in his jugular
Where love annunciates its name;

Will not admit magnificence
Which looms a startled blink away
To bleach with gold the retina
Resigned in arrogance to grey.

69

A GLEE AMONG THE GARRETS

[Emily Dickinson] mischievously said (of the Springfield *Republican*, edited by her friend, Samuel Bowles) "One of such papers as have nothing carnal in them."

Conrad Aiken

The poet is a menace to comformity...

Rollo May

Today the garrets are astir,
The scandal's quickly spread
By virtue overlaid with glee
While taking tea and bread.

Each lace jabot now wildly heaves,
Their cameos outraged —
To have that vile remark appear
Upon the printed page.

Purity is mortified,
Such wickedness long rankles;
The newspaper has dared imply
That women might have *ankles*!

The word like spice upon the lips —
Oh, dare we think it true?
What would become of womanhood
If everybody knew?

Calvin thundering in his grave!
Victoria in a pout!
And not a corset but is laced
To keep such rumours out;

Nor yet a whalebone stay but knows
Its dark atrocities:
The cost to what it guards is pain
And crimped velocities.

But soon the speculation's lynched
And buried out of town,
To rise some smiling Easter morn
And ring the era down.

A FEAST OF ABSENCE

When you had gone the love came in
As I supposed it would.
Only when the guest has gone
May host partake of food;

Before, is awed by nutriment
So lavishly arrayed —
Guest's absence a starvation
Were lone supping not delayed.

A feast of absence was my life,
"Farewells" the garnish given;
So feted, shall the epicure
Yet beg viands of heaven?

THE NILE

A woman died last week, young and in hope but a little while —
at the end of our garden. I thought since of the power of Death,
not upon affection, but its mortal signal. It is to us the Nile.

Emily Dickinson

Death is the silent, ruthless Nile —
The scaled beast it gives keep
Will, careless, swim its dark coil's length
Till sucked into its deep.

Who'd tell its gulping treachery,
Irrevocably gone —
While down indifferent centuries
The blanching Sphinx looks on

And none may pry her secrets —
Her reason overthrown —
The horror fixed her mindless stare
And sealed her lips with stone.

THE INFATUATION OF SAMENESS

I tell you what I see — the landscape of the spirit requires a lung,
but no tongue.

Emily Dickinson

Emily Dickinson I did like very much and do still, but she is rather
morbid and unnatural.

Joseph Lyman, 1858

[The legend of Emily Dickinson] takes its character mainly from the
romantic sorrows of a vivacious, witty young woman of distinguished family
who fell in love, suffered rejection, and spent the remainder of her life in
a white solitude that was, in the words of her finest biographer, George
Frisbie Whicher, "a long interval of sameness so absolute that the arrival
of a new month was like a guest's coming and the closed vans of a circus
passing her window at night seemed to her an Arabian experience."

John Malcolm Brinnin

It has been conjectured that after a conventional girlhood and a year
at Mount Holyoke Female Seminary she withdrew from the world into the
house of her austere father because of a blighted love affair. Whether or not
this is true hardly matters. The important fact is her choosing to live a life
that accords with Thoreau's advice to "Simplify, simplify, simplify," to
reach down to touch the bedrock of reality on which we stand.

Daniel G. Hoffman

A calendar of astonishment
Delineates my days
Which stretch before like untracked snow
No April could amaze

Nor June provoke to wonderment
Despite its humming green
Against a glacial consciousness
Where noiseless white is seen.

A voice might raise an iceberg
Whose bulk I scarce detect
To eliminate the echo,
As newer snow, defect;

Or whisper loose an avalanche
To blot the boisterous fool
Who'd mar the alpine altitude
Where ice and quiet rule.

And were there heard Arabia,
Malodorous and loud,
A scentless sleet would fast erase
Its clamour, as a shroud

Obliterates that human thing
Which squirmed in love or violence,
Commends it unidentified,
Unvoiced, to clay's blank silence.

An unmarked waste, horizonless,
Lies endless to my sight
And never vulgar sun offends
Its cool and chastening light

That infatuates with sameness
Till voiceless awe arises
And man nor beast nor living thing
But only white surprises;

And silence grows so absolute,
Untongued, the traveler pleads
To sight on steppe one perfect print
And stumble where it leads,

Spurred on by raucous ecstasy —
The only shout internal —
To sink into a waiting clasp,
Welcoming! Eternal!

NOTES FROM A YANKEE KITCHEN

In [Emily Dickinson's] best poems there is a mingling of the high diction of
theology with the low diction of the kitchen commonplace.

Daniel G. Hoffman

When I returned from where I'd been
I had outworn my life
So put it pensively aside
As cook the blunted knife.

I did not mourn the loss of it,
Another blade was given,
So bountifully does nature spend —
Or was the donor heaven?

Five empires withal expired
Then in a hard-reached drawer
I came upon the implement
Its use forgot, and power.

Neglect precipitates its rust,
I weigh its worth, a stranger,
Long puzzling why I hoard such tool —
The cutting edge! The danger!

NOT LEAST OF THREE

The mandible of life is Truth
And in this razored jaw
Truth's helpless worshippers succumb
Before they're eaten raw.

Beauty sets a kinder snare
Its martyrs will confess
Though incision by these talons
Proves lethal nonetheless.

I failed in Love's far subtler trap
My final hour was grim —
A trampling by roses,
A rending limb by limb.

A CAPABLE WOMAN

Wanted
To hire a girl or woman who is capable of doing the
entire work of a small family.

Newspaper advertisement placed by
Emily Dickinson's father

A warmhearted sturdy young immigrant, one of the "despised" Irish who were
then settling in America in large numbers, filled the position in March 1869.
Margaret Maher, just past twenty, became the mainstay of the family and
remained till after Emily's death. Mr. Jay Leyda comments: "How often
Emily must have looked at Maggie as a fellow exile, for community snobbery
was directed as much against the 'lower class' Irish as against the 'upper
class' Dickinsons, especially that queer writing woman! . . . they were willing
to believe any gossip or 'revelations' about the Dickinson sisters: madness
was one of the gentler accusations."

Maggie's letters written in phonetic spelling in a rustic hand have
miraculously survived and tell much about her character: "I dont want to
disapoint any person or Brake my word if i be Poor and working for my
living I will alway try to do rite. . . " (March 2, 1869). Her letters were often
signed "Miss Emily's and Vinnia's Maggie." "Emily Dickinson seemed never
to tire of defining Maggie's virtues and qualities for herself as well as for her
friends," Mr. Leyda observes. "To Mrs. Holland she wrote, 'Maggie, good
and noisy, the North Wind of the family, but sweets without a salt would
at last cloy. . . ' and 'Maggie is with us still, warm and wild and mighty.' "

All Ireland's weather in her face,
Its courage in her chin,
And all its music in her throat,
She calmly looks at him

With such an ancient dignity
As only suffering breeds,
Politely tells her history,
Describes her simple needs

And such vitality exudes
As stirs the very walls,
A strength the storms of Ireland forged
With drenching, stinging squalls.

And now the house reshapes itself
To meet this vibrant force;
I'll cook and moind me manners, sir,
And tend the girls, of course.

A northern season comes to stay!
A tempest domiciled!
But well I mark her quick-changed wind,
Salubrious and mild.

Unconcealed her hemispheres,
Her temperate warming streams,
All foretold in earnest face,
Its balance and extremes.

Stout faithfulness had rarely worn
A more endearing frame
Nor had love more rustic residence —
Nor exile less acclaim.

A kindred stuff makes up this soul;
I recognize my twin —
New England's weather in my face,
Its courage in my chin.

*. . . The kingdom of heaven is
like to a grain of mustard seed,
which a man took, and sowed in
his field: Which indeed is the
least of all seeds: but when it
is grown, it is the greatest
among herbs, and becometh a tree,
so that the birds of the air come
and lodge in the branches thereof.*

Matthew 13:31, 32

Heaven is large, is it not? Life is short too,
isn't it? Then when one is done, is there not
another, and — and — then if God is willing, we
are neighbours then.

Emily Dickinson

PART THREE:

AUTUMN SONG 1870-1879

*O Offspring of Dust! Be not content
with the ease of a passing day, and
deprive not thyself of everlasting rest.
Barter not the garden of eternal
delight for the dust-heap of a mortal
world. Up from thy prison ascend unto
the glorious meads above, and from thy
mortal cage wing thy flight unto the
paradise of the Placeless.*

Bahá'u'lláh

AUTUMN SONG

Odours tangled in the trees,
The sky was full of south,
Leaves raced headlong on the lawn,
One rose to kiss my mouth.

Its taste was tart as memory,
Its aroma was goodbye,
I felt a soft astonishment
It should so gladly die.

Immortality was hinted
In its flutter at my lip
Not one shrewd foot in sure pursuit
But cautious lest it slip.

THE KEY OF THE KINGDOM

Perhaps you laugh at me! Perhaps the whole United States are laughing
at me too! *I* can't stop for that! *My* business is to love...

...I feel as the band does before it makes its first shout.... Blessed
are they that play, for theirs is the kingdom of heaven.

Emily Dickinson

Today I want to dance and sing
And shed both shoe and hat;
Though papa flush and mamma blush,
I cannot stop for that.

Today I want to shout my joy —
The only listeners, trees;
And should the steeple look askance,
I'd seize it for trapeze.

Today I want to prink the town
And deck it with elation;
Though all the village raise alarm,
I'd garland next the nation.

Today I'd ask the world to tea
And have it stay to chat;
And should it laugh behind its hand,
I cannot stop for that.

Today I'd toast my old beau, Death —
Concealing my disdain.
Were Immortality his suit,
I'd bid the rogue remain.

THE FIGURE IN WHITE

For the last fifteen years of her life [from 1871 till her death in 1886] the village knew Emily Dickinson only as a white figure flitting about the garden in the summer dusk, as a voice from the dimness of the hall startling visitors in the Dickinson parlor by spectral interjections, or as a presence responding to occasion for congratulation or condolence by neighbourly gifts of flowers and dainties accompanied by little notes pencilled in an odd hand and phrased in orphic idiom.

George Frisbie Whicher

We are told that once a year she met the local world at a reception in her father's house, but sometimes sat with her face averted from the company in another room.

William Dean Howells

Year by year the area of her interest narrowed; year by year her indifference to the outer world grew more arctic. Now she dressed only in white, ventured less and less, and finally not at all, from her home; saw fewer friends, and, at last, none. . . . Long before her death she had become an Amherst legend; the woman in white; the eccentric recluse; the half-cracked daughter of Squire Dickinson.

Robert N. Linscott

If heaven were a league away
I would retire there
And beg a modest lodging,
Pull close to hearth my chair;

But found nearby a hidden lodge
Where I may bide in peace —
Though, curious, some try the door
The latch will not release.

The address none may know or guess,
And none obtain the key;
Each village keeps a benign witch,
Each house a mystery.

So, spectral in the hallway's gloom
I might call out to guest
As though a tentacle had stretched
To fathom foreign depth.

Or in the garden, dim as moth,
May flitter past rude gaze;
A gossip's sentence snaps in half,
Quick-mending to amaze.

But swiftly to my room repair
In space where none may see,
Draw my chair beside the fire and
Gather silence to me.

I wind my thoughts in knotless skein,
Unspoken, mile by mile, —
A league from immortality
Lay down my wool and smile.

RECIPE

I saw your Mrs. H._____. She looks a little tart, but Vinnie says makes excellent pies after one gets acquainted.

Emily Dickinson

Dear Children,

A firmness in the set of jaw,
A flintiness of eye,
Suggest the apple's more to taste
If baked into a pie.

A militancy of bearing,
A piquancy of stride,
Might slowly-stewed acquaintanceship
Reveal sweet pulp inside?

A tart and stinging way of speech,
A manner overbright —
If one likes apples well enough
Long cooking rewards bite!

Emily

THE VICIOUS VISITOR

The will is always near, dear, though the feet vary. The terror of the winter
has made a little creature of me, who thought myself so bold. Father was very
sick. I presumed he would die, and the sight of his lonesome face all day was
harder than personal trouble.

Emily Dickinson

I've had a curious winter, very swift, sometimes sober, for I haven't felt
well, much, and March amazes me! I didn't think of it much, that's all! . . . It
is easier to look behind at a pain, than to see it coming.

Emily Dickinson

If that grey hulk were merely Death,
I'd square with desolation —
His talent only that to free
His prey from isolation.

I've studied this oaf's vaunted skill
And marked a kindness there;
His lenient blow but sunders cage
That bird may take to air.

A greater menace lumbers now
With sinister design,
More fearsome for its formlessness
Which wraps the prey to dine

Stickily — to pulp the bones
And leave the very soul
Limp and mucilaginous;
And yet the victim, whole,

Endures to see the belching mass
Reluctantly depart
Without remorse that in its maw
It bears the viscid heart.

Then courageless, enfeebled,
The stunned thing in the cage
Turns lifelessly to life again
As one away an age,

Estranged from life's compelling thrust,
Its rude velocity,
And cautious sings, but ever fears
That grey ferocity

Which tore the pinion of its hope
And sucked the pap of will —
Its heinousness to ground the game
It won't in mercy kill.

FATHER

Father does not live with us now—he lives in a new house.
Though it was built in an hour, it is better than this...

Emily Dickinson

In April last, while father lived,
He crept out in the cold
And fed with grain the famished birds —
I'd not the heart to scold.

His slipper-shod shy charity,
A balm for me and birds;
I knew his pure and terrible heart
Spoke more in deeds than words.

A sorrow most resembles love,
It leaves the heart inflamed;
Ours eased because he fled our grasp
Accepted and unblamed.

Your letter brought his April back;
I sigh to see it pass
And mourn the unexpressed we lose
Each time we part the grass.

Emily

PROTECTION

[My father's] heart was pure and terrible, and I think no other like it exists.

Emily Dickinson

No cold intention I gave birth
Deprived the bird of breath;
Though I enticed it to my hand
I did not plot its death.

It throbbed ungoverned in my grasp —
The jailers feel it still;
Marked I how soft the small machine
That houses steely will.

Dread unmalleability —
Unfathomably strong —
To veer it recklessly toward life
Where lurk alarm and wrong.

The perilous, stubborn choice it makes
It could not understand.
In fear I clenched my trenchant fist
Who died within your hand.

THE WORD

We must be careful what we say. No bird resumes its egg.

Emily Dickinson

We must be careful what we say!
No word can be recalled
And once expressed reverberates
And we may stand appalled

And wish it back or wish it dead
Or gaze alarmed that we,
In domestic inattention,
Invoked a mystery

Which so reverses all we know
And all that is or seems,
We view our life across a chasm,
Inscrutable as dreams

That trail us with faint messages
Of haunting imprecision.
I once said *love* — my tongue turned stone;
I cannot ask revision.

RETURN OF THE DOVE

Mother went rambling, and came in with a burdock on her shawl, so we know that the snow has perished from the earth. Noah would have liked mother.

Emily Dickinson

Our gentle mother softly rose
To stroll the shivering fields,
Surveying the relentless strength
The fist of winter wields

And argued in her quiet way
For spring's delayed debut,
The advocate applauded by
Trees eager to renew.

The japonica looked hopefully on,
The cold hills stamped their feet;
The birds ignored the crust to hear
Would whiteness now retreat.

The crocus stretched, suppressed a yawn —
Chilled silence was retort;
But mother's shawl cheered all the ark
With burdock's terse report.

CRADLE SONG

Little Irish Maggie [Magaret Kelley] went to sleep at six o'clock, just the
time Grandpa rises, and will rest in the grass at Northampton tomorrow.
She has had a hard sickness, but her awkward little life is saved and
gallant now. Our Maggie [Margaret Maher] is helping her mother put
her in the cradle.

Emily Dickinson

A little child is laid to rest,
Heaven sent, heaven blest,
Pillowed gently, not to waken,
Heaven lent, heaven taken.

How green the coverlet of grass
Which none disturbs though centuries pass.
Note how still the cradle lies,
How small a space it occupies.

Whisper softly as you cross
Where her marker gathers moss.
Observe her interrupted dates!
Reflect that death abbreviates!

How young the babe, how long her sleep!
Heaven sent, heaven keep.
Warmly snuggled in the ground,
Heaven lent, heaven bound.

NEAR AND FAR

Remoteness founds a poignancy
Whose message is unclear;
Low-whispered, garbled, urgent, floats
Dim meaning to our ear.

But nearness has the fearsome skill
To speak in lucid tone
And cleave the soul and deafen ear
And turn the limbs to stone.

FRIENDSHIP

To multiply the harbours
Does not reduce the sea;
My little ship love-laden goes —
Returns an argosy.

And though it finds in every port
Both refuge and fair trade
I'd wish the ocean narrower
And ships less frailly made.

CAROL

Exultant shepherds bear the news
That laid in straw was found
A Gift that would renew the earth
Should gratitude abound.

Pass the Gift from hand to hand,
Deplore its rustic beauty;
In mockery fix it to a tree,
Revile it as a duty.

Reject the workmanship as flawed,
Despise its frugal cost
Unworthy of our jaded taste,
Regard it soon as lost.

On unmarked spot near Calvary
Indifference lays a stone,
Reciprocating Gift of gifts —
The worth to Giver known.

Unostentatious is the rock
Whose rude weight naught will lift.
Smile down on our economy —
Sweet Child, accept our gift.

THE SUMMIT

I hope that you are well, and nothing mars your peace but its divinity—
for ecstasy is peril.

Emily Dickinson

Experiment gives stimulus —
Enough to wither fear;
The usual fosters caution
Which guides the foot to veer.

Teased by sharp curiosity
I clambered to the ledge;
Closed to me was safe return,
The height dulled bravery's edge.

The hawk's dark wings here brush my cheek,
Strange winds pull at my hair;
Whose voice dissolved the path I took
And bids me step on air?

SIGHT

The unknown is the largest need of the intellect,
though for it no one thinks to thank God...

Emily Dickinson

The finite we can scrutinize,
The infinite suspect;
And though its emblems singe my eyes
Its outlines I detect.

Should staring cost my shabby sight
And ruin my seldom one
I'll seek its contours with delight,
My hands outstretched in sun.

My pantry eyes thus burned away
And those more rarely used
I'll stroke infininty one day
Acceptably excused.

93

STRAWBERRIES

Dr. Stearns died homelike...

Emily Dickinson

Eliza brings the strawberries —
Fresh, aswim in cream —
The patient's waking whim to flesh
The taste he'd chased in dream.

A homelike tableau! By the bed
The hushed Eliza stands,
Extends the tempting blood-red fruit —
The sleeper has no hands.

The stopped clock still as Judgment Day,
The girl as still as wood,
And in the dead-white crockery bowl,
Athrob with life, the food.

LOVE'S FARE

The martyr may not choose his food
But gourmand won't complain
If cup holds only suffering
And plate be heaped with pain.

The tart fare, tribulation,
His appetite but whets,
Each lavish course a banquet whose
Swift passage he regrets.

Consumed is each least morsel —
Crumb, stem, stone, rind and all,
The victuals of love's festal board
Were ever sugared gall.

Were final wine a scarlet brew
He'll drain the keg, if able,
And rising long embrace sweet Host
Who sets so rich a table.

THE SPELL

Life holds us in exquisite spell —
The spider's shoe might shake it;
But seething dark conspiracies
Swarm unseen to break it —

A dingy knowing violates
Our sun, our peach, our day;
And though we clasp a friend's warm hand
Its comfort's that of clay.

THE FEW

When I lost the use of my eyes, it was a comfort to think that there were
so few real books that I could easily find one to read me all of them.

Emily Dickinson

In silence I select the books
And come to understand
The ones I'd choose to shelve my mind
Are counted on one hand —

Their speaking power so intense
The reader, eye or ear,
Receives, unmasked, communicant
And neither is in fear

That all should be revealed this way —
A private truth confessed
Which garbed in sombre raiment yet
Will leave both souls undressed —

That mind to mind and soul to soul
Two privacies unravel,
Oblivious to the teeming shelf
Where leathers preen and babble.

THE DWELLING

I do not care for the body, I love the timid soul, the blushing, shrinking soul;
it hides for it is afraid...
Each of us gives or takes heaven in corporeal person, for each of us has the
skill of life.

Emily Dickinson

That sorrow have a place to dwell
And joy a home be given,
God first created fiery hell
And then made placid heaven.

Willing them cohabit in peace
He built a simple frame,
Installed the warring occupants
And gave it flesh as name.

God really does not need such house
Except His powers display,
That under one frail common roof
Two opposing forces stay.

The dwelling is dispensable —
He builds it for a day,
Demolishes at sundown, snatches
Shivering mouse away.

Or possibly He gives the home
That suffering unfold
And, reconciled, the lovers wed
And love's triumph be told.

The Architect designs the house
That peace have roof and eaves.
The passions that have stormed its walls
The mouse observes, but leaves.

THE BELLE

When her hand was attuned to her spirit [Emily Dickinson] worked in the harmony of genius that makes its own world and produces things of absolute individuality.... Her kind of domestic mysticism would have gone for little in the world's eyes had she not from her early years shown that she possessed that angelic familiarity with language that defines the poet.

John Malcolm Brinnin

The relentless music's torment
Dooms as it redeems,
Propelling the breathless dancer
Half-swooning toward a dream

That would not have the music cease,
That sweeps away the hall
And leaves the dancer panting,
The sole guest at the ball —

The orchestra dispersed or fled,
Courteous partner gone;
Just the harrying harmony
And at the window dawn.

No pause to ease the ankle,
No fan to cool flushed cheek,
The awesome music swelling
And then a voice: *Child, speak!*

CLOCKS

The only clock I had was fear
To regulate my hours,
So made a timepiece of my own
From that assigned to flowers.

With all my mornings April
And summer my high noon,
Existence dawdled pleasantly
But expired leaves too soon

Announced a shadowed hour of
Fast-ticking dark despair —
That meridian should falter
And clocks fail all repair.

A kinder dial now governs me
To softly pare my day;
What time? my soul, impatient, asks —
It's ten of life, I say.

THE RUNAWAY

A little boy [Jerry Scannell, age fourteen] ran away from Amherst a few days ago, and when asked where he was going, replied, "Vermont or Asia." Many of us go farther. My pathetic Crusoe—

Emily Dickinson

Are you certain there is another life? When overwhelmed to know, I fear that few are sure.

Emily Dickinson

What distance, sir, to far away?
That's where I plan to run.
I reason there's a sky there, too,
And possibly a sun.

Vermont and Asia sound remote
And dangerous on the tongue,
But I am brave and capable
And strong of limb and lung.

And I shall have adventures there,
See wondrous and strange things.
I'll slay a dragon if I must
And be the guest of kings.

A princess will attract my heart
And by one valiant deed
I shall prove worthy of her love
And on my snow-white steed

We'll ride through cool green forests
To Maine or Zanzibar
And build our Kingdom by the sea.
Tell me, sir, how far?

LAVINIA'S SONG

Vinnie is happy with her duties, her pussies, and her posies, for the little garden within, though tiny, is triumphant...

When the flowers annually died and I was a child, I used to read Dr. Hitchcock's book on the "Flowers of North America." This comforted their absence, assuring me they lived...

Emily Dickinson

The song in summer has a swell
That dulls our darker knowing
When fecundity's green evidence
Riotously showing

And wingéd, buzzing, teeming life
In field, on bough, in stream
Persuade in rapt hyperbole
Abundance were no dream.

Our caution cushioned, we accept
Irrefutable brief
And preen as indestructible —
Then falls the frost-maimed leaf;

And though we coax it tenderly
Or seek art of repair
Its plunge portends — ah, bittersweet! —
A spring renewed elsewhere.

THE TENANT

When her mother was on a visit to Boston, Lavinia Dickinson wrote to her saying, "Pussy is pretty comfortable. Emily entraps a mouse every night."

Some hearts keep kettles on the boil
For any vagrant guest;
Some have doors wide and welcoming,
Inviting: enter! rest!

Ubiquitous, the resident!
Love makes in each his home
And pleads to tenant mine as well
Although its walls are stone

And all within is dank and dark
And none is offered bed.
Insistent Love protests all's well
Where rests his exiled head.

In most unlikely wainscots lives
That miracle, the mouse,
Its scampering the home's sole life.
Come, Love, invade this house

And while stern mind, the landlord, sleeps
And Tabby dozes purring,
Let your ardent, gleeful capers tell:
All's well! Here Love is stirring!

THE INTERVIEW

... on August 16, 1870, I [Higginson] found myself face to face with my
hitherto unseen correspondent... this interview left our relation very
much as it was before;—on my side an interest that was strong and
even affectionate, but not based on any thorough comprehension.... [She
wore] white piqué with a blue net worsted shawl.... She came toward me
with two day-lillies, which she put in a childlike way into my hand,
saying softly, under her breath, "These are my introduction."... When I
said, at parting, that I would come again some time, she replied, "Say
in a long time; that will be nearer. Some time is no time." We met
only once again [on December 3, 1873], and I have no express record
of that visit.

T. W. Higginson

I crossed the room with flowers
As, curious, he stood;
And knew I need not fear this man
Whose solemn heart was good.

I answered with demureness
The questions that he put
But realization quickly came —
He would not grasp my root

Which plunges in voraciousness
To gather what it earns
Where civility's conventions
The soil not overturns.

The afternoon politely spent,
He bowed and left the room —
As bewildered by the lilies
As by obscurer bloom.

THE FOURTH OF JULY

Did you know there had been a fire here, and that but for a whim of the wind Austin and Vinnie and Emily would have all been homeless? ... I sprang to the window, and each side of the curtain saw that awful sun. The moon was shining high at the time, and the birds singing like trumpets.... And so much lighter than day was it, that I saw a caterpillar measure a leaf far down in the orchard; and Vinnie kept saying bravely, "It's only the fourth of July."

Emily Dickinson

The mother sleeping guiltlessly,
Hushed daughters creep around
Awed by what their window tells —
Damnation come to town!

Congregationalist horror!
The townsfolk rush about
In moist and fervid righteousness
To keep Damnation out.

All their fears are manifest
In hot forked tongues of fire —
Here proof of Satan's subtle scheme,
His ardent, vile desire!

Each barn and horse and house astir!
Each frightened tree stock still!
Damnation dancing everywhere
With diabolic will.

One girl would hold to all she knows,
This hell too close, too real,
Secures our peace against a light
Which starker truth reveals

And sweeps red carnage from our mind
That, safe, we take to bed
In gossamer assurance:
Such fireworks! she said.

Can a bird fall in a snare upon
the earth, where no gin is for him!
Shall one take up a snare from the
earth, and have taken nothing at all!

Amos 3:5

We dignify our faith when we can cross the
ocean with it, though most prefer ships.

Emily Dickinson

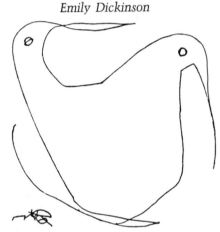

PART FOUR:

WINTER SONG 1880-1886

O Son of Spirit! The bird seeketh its
nest; the nightingale the charm of the
rose; whilst those birds, the hearts of
men, content with transient dust, have
strayed far from their eternal nest, and
with eyes turned towards the slough of
heedlessness are bereft of the glory of the
divine presence. Alas! How strange and
pitiful; for a mere cupful, they have
turned away from the billowing seas of
the Most High, and remained far from the
most effulgent horizon.

Bahá'u'lláh

WINTER SONG

Peace is such a deep place
And life so small a spoon
Though we dig with fervour
We cannot reach it soon.

Heaven's such a high place
And shank of hope so short
Though we jump forever
'Tis unrewarded sport.

Winter's such a cold place,
Igniting faith an art,
I clasp my warming vision
Of the swift thaw of the heart.

FRAGMENT

I gnaw on absence like a bone;
The nutriment it gives
Suffices desiccated heart
Which though it faints yet lives.

Penury asked a richer meal
But beggar knows content;
If there be tossed a crust to him
He blesses the intent,

Conjectures loaf it's token of —
Stoutened courage bristling,
His want concealed, he owns the street:
Step proud, head high, whistling.

THE GUEST

The stranger, death, is much revered
When he is but a guest.
Inhabiting the mind's spare room
His sacred tenure's blessed.

When he becomes our noisy kin,
Assuming family parlour,
Profane grows the familial tie —
Domestic, our ardour.

Nothing dissolves our noisome bond
Except eternity;
I close the shutters, shun the crowd,
Death too much mob for me.

THE EMPRESS

[Emily Dickinson's] legend does not conveniently accommodate the
outsize "Empress of Calvary" ...

John Malcolm Brinnin

Of the thorn, dear, give it to me, for I am strongest. Never carry what
I can carry.... What I would I cannot say in so small a place.

Emily Dickinson

Give all your piercing thorns to me,
My sinew grown stronger
By gash, upon a daunting hill,
Where needles wound the longer.

Assign to me what I may hold
For something straightens me;
The weightlessness of innocence
My arms learned from a tree.

108

TUNE FOR A FIDDLE

We had another fire—it was in Phoenix Row, Monday a week ago, at two in the night.... The brook from Pelham saved the town.... The fire-bells are oftener now, almost, than the church-bells. Thoreau would wonder which did the most harm...

Emily Dickinson

Stay all the bells lest Thoreau hear
And castigate the Parson,
Or write a windy treatise
On the incidence of arson.

The transcendentalist is soon
Provoked to agitation,
Beware the irked philosopher
Disturbed in meditation.

Desist from clanging! Halt the din!
Forbid your fears to churn.
Join hands with Thoreau, levitate —
And let the village burn.

But should it threaten Phoenix Row,
Preserve the petty cash;
Then play the fiddle, confident
The bird will rise from ash.

STORM

No verse in the Bible has frightened me so much from a child as "from him that hath not, shall be taken even that he hath." Was it because its dark menace deepened our own door?

Emily Dickinson

I shall not venture out today
Unless the skies relent
Their wild and gnashing anguish to
Grant life sun's consent.

There may pass this frantic keening,
Hysteria of rain;
What tyrannical power
Assails ether with pain

As to cancel its avowal,
Withdraw its bridal *yes*?
Inconsolably lamenting,
I'd make a widow's guess.

Such persuasive desolation!
Such conviction in the storm!
How inform the lonely orphan
Redoubtable is dawn?

THANKSGIVING
1882

In spite of her isolation, [Emily Dickinson] was solicitous of village life, held it closely in her attention long after she had ceased to be part of it, and observed it constantly from behind the curtains of her window and the hedges of her garden.

John Malcolm Brinnin

While others go to church, I go to mine.... I hope your Thanksgiving was not too lonely, though if it were, affection must not be displeased. Sue sent me a lovely banquet of fruit which I sent to a dying Irish girl in our neighbourhood. That was my Thanksgiving. Those that die are near me because I lose my own—not all my own, thank God. A darling "own" remains, more darling than I name.

Emily Dickinson

Thanksgiving, and the table sighs
Banked high with evidence
That our simple twelvemonth labour
Secures munificence.

The ritual of gratitude
Enacted once again
Confirms that pilgrim voyagers
Sight bounty now, as then.

One drops her work as by impulse
To journey from her breath,
Her *thank-you* unrehearsed, unheard,
Across the chasm, death.

HARVEST

Much comes later, like the peach
Which shuns the tree's debut
And then appears in gratitude
For what a sun can do.

I scrutinize light warily
To see were power able
To fructify the chary soul
To deck a higher table.

STORE

With a to-morrow in its cupboard, who would be "an hungered?"

Emily Dickinson

A Tomorrow in the cupboard,
A shelf stocked with Belief,
Who would be an hungered?
Who, fasting, waste with grief?

An Eternity in mothballs,
A Promise in the drawer,
Who might decline to banquet?
What glutton ask for more?

Triumph sealed in canisters,
Glassed conserves of Delight,
Who would want for laughter
Or fear famine born of blight?

A cellar of Yea Verily
That never vintner sold,
A silo cramfull of Thou Art,
An orchard of Behold.

A Fulfilment in the larder
To batten the most lean,
How perverse the starving
Who will not sup on dream!

A Surely tied in ribbons,
Hope's harvest on the vine,
Well nurtured are the faithful;
How sumptuously they dine!

THE CITIZEN

To venture is to change one's sky;
To love, change hemisphere.
My own is but minutest world,
Its population dear.

And some I love inhabit skies
Where planets churn and toss;
None might have wished to leave me but
There came a plague of loss.

I'm doubly a citizen —
My loves are my estate —
And might I not in either sphere
Find welcome at the gate?

Though each realm yields a universe
But one assures delight;
I stretch my arch but dare not choose —
My poise, retreat or flight?

MOTHER

I hoped to write you before, but mother's dying almost stunned my spirit...

Emily Dickinson

Dear Cousins,

To value is a jeopardy,
Naught but the precious harms;
If detachment not be mastered
A loss creates alarms.

Pain's puzzling mission ratified,
Our mother slipped away
To drift into the infinite —
How brief a snowflake's day!

Persistently pain cultivates
A tenderness unknown,
Thus we lost a larger mother
Than any we had owned.

Her retreat achieved in beauty,
That solemn artist, death,
Left her portrait on the pillow —
Detail complete, save breath.

Emily

INTIMATIONS

The past is not a package
The mind can put away
As lover would a letter
To review on loveless day.

The future's not divine report
To scrutinize at leisure
But taps events along the spine,
The swift news doom or pleasure.

Eternity is not a shout
Nor sinister like whisper.
While strolling once through my awed soul
I overheard its vesper.

Heaven's not a smart far place
Small homely things announce it
Joy occupies the environs —
Should pain, shall I renounce it?

WITCHCRAFT

I would like to learn. Could you tell me how to grow, or is it unconveyed, like melody or witchcraft?

Emily Dickinson

Many of [Emily Dickinson's] finest works have the quality of outrage packed into formal disposition of words and all but stifled in the process. She is [sometimes] the demonic artist in fury, wrenching the tight meters and neat figures of her characteristic language in order to come upon utterance adequate to her anguish.

John Malcolm Brinnin

... She is the poet of the inscrutable necessity which we endure... there was no theorist of poetry to prepare the public for Emily Dickinson's originality; her verse had to win its own readers. It has forced them to redefine their notions of poetry to include her poems.

Daniel G. Hoffman

... In an earlier time, Dickinson would have been burned as a witch, for she spoke in tongues and she spoke against authority. She is not only the poet of consciousness, the register of that mysterious interaction between the inner self and the world of nature, but the poet who set herself against religious orthodoxy, the social order, and the poetic standards of her time.

Louise Bernikow

To offer and withhold the breast
Is woman's only power;
To lay the meal and call the men
Invests her for an hour

With all the kingdom she's allowed,
A brief and sovereign sway;
My breast untapped, no kitchen mine,
Yet I shall find a way.

For other powers roil in me —
Unchecked, would scald with rage;
Aproned in meek gingham poise
I set my pen to page

And not a witch who ever burned
But lends her skill to me.
I tip my furious cauldron
And set their spirits free.

HIGGINSON'S CHOICE

From [Higginson's] choice of her poems one can gauge the preference of the time for narrative moralizing poems on such topics as "Life," "Nature," "Love" and "Death." Under such rubrics, and under poem titles of his own composition, Higginson presents his poetess, only by degrees moving the reader toward the disquieting surprises of a poem like "Safe in their alabaster chambers."

Daniel G. Hoffman

[Emily Dickinson] that prolific writer of notes of condolence...

Northrop Frye

... Love is that one perfect labour naught can supersede. I suppose the pain is still there, for pain that is worthy does not go so soon.... Put it out of your hearts, children. Faith is too fair to taint it. Love will not expire. There was never an instant when it was lifeless in the world...

Emily Dickinson

... of all great poets, she is the most lacking in taste; there are innumerable beautiful lines and passages wasted in the desert of her crudities; her defects, more than those of any other great poet that I have read, are constantly at the brink, or pushing beyond the brink, of her best poems.

Yvor Winters

Death cannot plunder half so fast
As fervour can re-earn;
Engaged in love's employment
It magnifies return.

Though stealthy, swift and rude the hand
That rifles all our gains,
Loss compounds abundance,
By mandamus all remains.

Fervour summons lasting wealth
Earth lends but heaven stores —
Death that bank's mere messenger
Who cannot pass its doors.

The daring theft is bungled —
Vigilant faith frustrates;
For love is never destitute
While heaven compensates.

CONVERSATION

The temperature of other minds —
How new and strange an awe!
My own words chill and burn me
Chafing my brain raw.

Moderate words from lips of guests
Alarm — as zephyr blown —
One whom extremes have nourished
But was not quite alone;

One who conversed in accents
Temperate tongues disown —
The delirium of fever,
The chink of frozen bone.

THE LESSON

Anecdotes relating to [Emily Dickinson's] mischievousness, her wit, her waywardness, are not enough.... We like to know ... that even when her solitude was most remote she was in the habit of lowering from her window, by a string, small baskets of fruit or confectionery for children. But there are other things we should like to know much more. There seems now, however, little likelihood of our ever learning anything more...

Conrad Aiken

The children's eyes grow round and wise,
Their exclamations ring,
That manna should be basketed
And lowered by a string.

I'd entice their confirmation
That though the source be far,
Incredibly the suppliants' hope
Brings bounty where they are.

I'd have these famished pilgrims learn
What weak thread bears delight —
No heart without its desert,
Its weary Israelite;

How mute prayer will yield oasis
In monotony of drouth
And faith's shy intermittent plea
Place honey in the mouth;

And miracles grow commonplace,
As homely as my twine,
While love waves from a window
As from a place divine.

THE SEAMSTRESS

It is love that threads my needle,
Affection braids the ply,
Faith's thimble nimbly shields from stab —
Thus swift my fingers fly

To stoutly reinforce the seam
Against death's careless rending;
My cunning stitch destructible
But heaven deft at mending.

THE HEARTH OF HEAVEN

In heaven's frigid corridors
Cold angels dine alone;
God's loneliness congeals desire
And chills aspiring bone.

Draught-swept divine remoteness
Refrigerates our awe
That the timid thermophilic soul
Precipitate heart's thaw

By the fire of its longing
And thus will conflagrate
And warm the lonely feet of God
At reunion's cheering grate

Where angels in their threadbare coats
Extol the willing flame
Which God — His hands outstretched to it —
Gives everlasting name.

REVENGE

...I grew very sick and gave the others much alarm... the doctor calls it "revenge of the nerves"; but who but Death has wronged them?

Emily Dickinson

How great the elasticity
Of chambers of the brain,
Accommodating in small cell
So huge a bulk as pain!

How deft the brain's facility
For storing and retrieving!
How prompt to activate the heart's
Capacity for grieving!

The efficiency is equal
When joy's the subject stowed,
But rattling in its dwarfing cell
Will languish and erode

For busy death will place such call
Upon the bustling brain,
Although review of bliss were asked
The heart will plead in vain.

THE BELOVED

While she wrote love poetry that indicates a strong attachment, it has proved impossible to know the object of it, or even how much of it was fed by her poetic imagination.

The New Columbia Encyclopedia

Certain poems exist which I find impossible to interpret except in terms of human, rather than divine, love. One such poem, written about 1882 ... [is] infinitely touching in what it reveals of the silent suffering of the woman behind the poems.

John Wain

... what is remarkable is that her withdrawal, although it began gradually, eventually became as total as a religious renunciation. And it is not an impossible hypothesis that the Beloved whose departure she mourns may not be a particular man but Christ, the loss of religious certainty, the Soul's lover.

Peter Jones

There is no hint of what turned her life in upon herself, and probably this was its natural evolution, or involution, from tendencies inherent in the New England, or the Puritan spirit... no doubt [poetry] was a radiant happiness in the twilight of her hidden, silent life.... We have never known the invisible and intangible ties binding all creation in one, so nearly touched as in [her poems].

William Dean Howells

I could not spell your name, my love;
No letters could contain you.
Embarrassed was the pen that tried
To address or to name you.

I could not paint your portrait, dear,
Whose face defied all palettes;
The shrinking brush, despairing hand,
Lacked craft to truly tell it.

I could not match your praise to song —
Unfit my voice and cadence,
Nor music ever was composed
Adequate to radiance.

Death came before I found the means
To spell or paint or sing you.
My silent soul which all inscribed
I hasten now to bring you.

POEM

I fashioned from my pain a poem,
Inscribed it on a page;
I used self-pity as my pen
And dipped the nib in rage.

The letters wept themselves away,
The sheet went blank with shame
And I could not recall the verse
Although my grief remained.

I made from hurt another song
And wrote in in the air;
My pen was formed of fortitude
My brilliant ink was prayer.

The letters set themselves aflame,
The page was upward flown,
By wind or heaven now perused —
To both the author's known.

CALLED

A word is inundation, when it comes from the sea.

Emily Dickinson

The shore is safer than the sea,
It does not seethe nor call
Nor buffet and betray who'd quest
Nor heinously appal.

Astute's the pilgrim on the land
Who never heeds the sea
And resolutely walks away —
It is not so with me.

I gaze upon the bitter wrecks
Mercilessly broken
And gauge my craft and weigh the words
The scheming waves have spoken.

124

A PAGEANT OF ALLEGIANCES

The instructions left by Emily Dickinson for her funeral sound like the directions for a pageant of allegiances. . . . She asked to be carried by the six Irish men she had known . . . out the back door, around through the garden, through the opened barn from front to back, and then through the grassy fields to the family plot, always in sight of the house.

Jay Leyda

I know the funeral I would choose —
A light solemnity;
Two Dennys, Stephen, Pat and Dan
And Tom to carry me.

Through the back door, slow of gait,
The boys will bear my shell
To traverse again the garden
Which I, when quick, knew well.

Then through the barn's broad wide-flung doors,
For though I then be mute,
The beasts and good scents biding there
I would again salute.

And crossing front to back the barn
The men will find the fields
I visited (more agilely!)
To learn what Nature yields.

And could they rest a moment there
The pausing were relief
And all the fading things I mourned
Should know my span was brief.

At last the family plot attained,
Strong arms lay me away
That husk begin its final task
And gently wilt to clay.

I know the funeral I would choose
When I forsake my room;
Tom Kelley and his stalwart five
Will guide me to the tomb.

A slow tour of allegiances
Past all I loved and knew,
While I in vast eternity
Smile down on the review.

NOTICE

There's something humble marrow knows
That's shy to meet the mind,
A subcutaneous wisdom
Brain's scalpel cannot find;

And, whispering, lifts the hackles,
Spells eviction to dense bone
To warn the tenant of smug flesh
To seek a fitter home.

LAST WORDS

The mist is rising
and I must go in. Called back, little ones.
The air like gingerbeer —
and God all morning
and naught will fail or fear —
the least, the least of sparrows
and there shall be no mourning —
and healed, healed all my sorrows —
and a rank, radiant as light,
a rank of angels —
Oh what a dear confusion!
but a life is such a little thing to lose —
and God's face bright, not angry,
I shall not scuff my toe and say You wronged me,
but joy and bells and ecstasy
and the gleaming City, white and past imagining,
a face at every window — God's Own face!
There was so much to love
even in my little world
and the smell of apples might detain me —
And labour put away, and pain,
an evanescent grace and June forever!
A waving hand — Oh, is it Jesus'?
The door where all attain all goodness,
where saints and children gather —
migration is a friendly flight —
but let there be alyssum with the balm
and damson and the wild daisy — even one! —
and love, unending love,
and never parting
and forgiveness like a flood —
and an early peach.
All is astonishment
and those I loved awaiting —
Oh this light unbearable!
It burns, it burns.

And the open door — I reach, I reach —
In the Lord put I my trust: how say ye to my soul,
Flee as a bird to your mountain!
Oh Father, calling, calling — and the light!
The light an immolation! *Unto Thee lift I up mine eyes . . .*
Oh this lifting, lifting —
lifting beyond sense,
past doubt and why and how!
Bright Presence, lift me now!

*Our soul is escaped as a bird out
of the snare of the fowlers: the
snare is broken, and we are escaped.*

Psalms 124:7

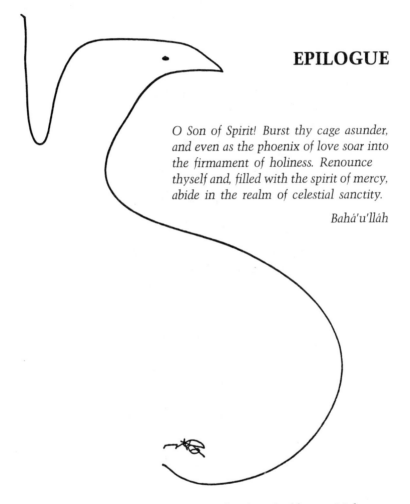

EPILOGUE

*O Son of Spirit! Burst thy cage asunder,
and even as the phoenix of love soar into
the firmament of holiness. Renounce
thyself and, filled with the spirit of mercy,
abide in the realm of celestial sanctity.*

Bahá'u'lláh

I believe that we shall in some manner be cherished by our Maker —
that One who gave us this remarkable earth has the power still
further to surprise that which He has caused. Beyond that all is
silence ...

Emily Dickinson

MAGGIE SAVES THE DAY

When Emily Dickinson's poems found an audience [some time after her death in 1886 of what was diagnosed as Bright's disease] and a photograph of her was needed, Maggie [Margaret Maher, the Irish servant] offered a daguerreotype that the family, including the sitter, had disliked and discarded. Without her love we would not have the only photographic image of a great poet.

Jay Leyda

Well, if you think, then, this will do
I'll give the lend of it;
But, sure, I'd hate it lost to me
And mind, don't go and bend it.

They didn't loik it, not at all,
And she the least, I'd say;
Give it me, then! I asked real bold,
Not me Sunday-parlour way.

I kept it on me chest of drawers —
Beg pardon! — *chiffonier* —
For comfort in the loss of her
Or when I'm taken queer.

Fond, I was, of all the lot,
Me being, loik, sentimental;
It's aisy seen I cover up
Y'might say, temperamental.

Miss Emily — well, there was a one
Whose loik I'd never seen,
And took her to me heart, I did,
Her treating me a queen.

And some in town mistaking her —
They thought her strange because...
Well, never mind — I seen and knew;
Why, half a saint she was.

When I'd not yet confessed me sins
And won a state of grace,
I'd lash the townsfold with me tongue
And tell them to their face.

So take it then, the loikness,
And print it with her verse,
Miss Emily, though — God rest her soul,
May reward me with a curse.

I don't know, meself, Posterity
On whose behalf you speak,
But hearing that you'll print the poems
I'm overcome all weak.

The town would be fair dumbstruck
To hear her praises sung
And that, sure, puts them in their place
Much better than me tongue.

I loik a poem meself, I do,
To charm ill-luck away —
And you that grateful! Me that proud!
Who'd think I'd save the day?

WHO?

When I state myself, as the representative of the verse, it does not mean me, but a supposed person.

Emily Dickinson

It is of course possible to draw inferences about the artist from the work of art and vice versa, but these inferences are never conclusive.

C. G. Jung
Psychology and Literature (1930)

Her poems tell it all, and what they say should be the final truth.

John Malcolm Brinnin

Not the poet but the poem.

Tagore

I was the girl in crimson silk
You clasped in your embrace,
But when you pressed your lips to hers
She did not have my face.

I was the austere cloistered one
You sighted from your carriage
Who when you called in courteous suit
Revealed another marriage.

I was the frivolous dainty belle
Beneath lace parasol,
But when you called to conquer her
It was not me at all.

I was the flitting, white-gowned girl
Whose garden at twilight
Contained her as a faint dim moth —
My voice belied your sight.

I was the wraith betrothed to Death
You'd rescue back to Life.
The laughing girl you told of this
You would not have for wife.

I was that one who spelled her love
In words that all might see,
But when your hot eye stripped the page
It read: Eternity.

After such knowledge, what forgiveness? [Emily Dickinson] looked into depths we can only just bear to know about, pushed against frontiers we shrank away from.... When we read her poems, we are in the presence of something as pure and cold as water that comes up from hundreds of feet deep in the rock.

John Wain

JUDGE TENDERLY

Shall I write
And not of thee through whom my fingers bend
To hold my quill?

George Herbert
1593-1633

My words were medicines to me
Who found no other balm,
For raging fevers clawed at me
And verse restored the calm.

My words were torn up by the roots,
In indignation wrenched
From the dark soil of a heart
That piercing knowledge drenched.

My words were cryptic, crudely formed,
Their drilling pace intense;
Say not I spoke inaudibly
Though firm my jaw was clenched.

My words were bullets aimed in haste,
Their purpose not to slay
But signal that I found retreat
In news a world away;

Were white flags raised on hope's rampart
So Immortality
Send Death to exculpate the crime
And set the exile free.

GENERAL NOTES

Letters of Emily Dickinson

Excerpts on the title and divider pages are from letters to: Holland, Autumn 1859 (title page); Root, May 7, 1850 (Part One); Norcross, May 1863 (Part Two); Holland, 1853 (Part Three); Turner, 1859 (Part Four); Norcross, November 1882 (Epilogue).

In instances where specific letters suggested a poem or were, for mood, consulted, the date and name of the recipient is given in "Notes on the Poems" on pages 136-142, unless identified in the epigraph. Information about the recipients is given under "Correspondents" on page 18.

Quotations from Bahá'u'lláh

The quotations of Bahá'u'lláh used on the title and divider pages are from His mystical composition, *The Hidden Words*, written *circa* 1858 on the banks of the Tigris in Baghdad, after He had left His native Persia.

Jacket and Divider Page Drawings

Tsepohr ("Bird"), by Yisraela Uzziel, age five, of Haifa, Israel, used by permission of Mr. and Mrs. Jacob Uzziel.

NOTES ON THE POEMS

PART ONE: SPRING SONG

Spring Song. E.D. to Samuel Bowles, Spring 1862.

May One Waltz? E.D. to Abiah Root, May 7, 1845.

Bread. E.D. to Abiah Root, 1845. Emily Dickinson's bread won a prize of 75¢ in the Annual Cattle Show of 1857 and she served as judge in successive shows, Division of Rye and Indian Bread.

The Prisoner. E.D. to Abiah Root, May 16, 1848; to L. and F. Norcross, 1864.

Home. Sweet Home. E.D. to Abiah Root, January 17, 1848.

Valentine. E.D. to Austin Dickinson, February 1848; to L. and F. Norcross, 1870.

Prayer. E.D. to Abiah Root, May 7, 1850.

Veteran. E.D. to Abiah Root, May 7, 1850.

Thanksgiving: 1851. E.D. to Austin Dickinson, November 17, 1851.

Sawdust. E.D. to Austin Dickinson, July 5, 1851; to Austin Dickinson (undated) 1851.

Contempt. E.D. to Austin Dickinson, April 1853.

Abraham and the Nightingale. E.D. to Austin Dickinson, July 5, 1851. Jenny Lind (born Johanna Maria and latterly known as Madame Jenny Lind-Goldschmidt) was a Swedish soprano, unrivaled master of coloratura; she was known as "the Swedish Nightingale." After retiring from the operatic stage in 1849 she devoted herself to concert singing and oratorio. In 1850-52 she was engaged to sing on tour in American by P. T. Barnum.

The Traveler. E.D. to Austin Dickinson, June 1853.

Three Words. E.D. to Dr. and Mrs. J. G. Holland, 1858.

Hope. E.D. to Dr. and Mrs. J. G. Holland, Autumn 1859.

One. E.D. to Elizabeth Holland, Autumn 1859.

Ladies' Verse. I – E.D. to Dr. and Mrs. J. G. Holland, 1853; II – to Mary Bowles, 1859.

The Sermon. E.D. to Dr. and Mrs. J. G. Holland, 1854.

Emily's Song. E.D. to Samuel Bowles, 1858: "In such a porcelain life one likes to be *sure* that all is well lest one stumble upon one's hopes in a pile of broken crockery."

The Old Suitor. E.D. to Elizabeth Holland, late Summer 1856.

Moving House. E.D. to Dr. J. G. Holland, 1856.

Forever Now. E.D. to Elizabeth Holland, Summer 1856.

The Democrat. E.D. to Dr. and Mrs. J. G. Holland, 1858.

Promenade. E.D. to Samuel Bowles, 1858. Gen. 17.5: Abraham, "father of many." Abraham's bosom is a synonym for heaven to some Christians and Jews: Luke 16:22-31.

A Modest Glass. E.D. to L. Norcross, 1859.

PART TWO: SUMMER SONG

Summer Song. E.D. to L. and F. Norcross, 1861.

The Caller. E.D. to Mary Bowles, 1861.

The Criminal. E.D. to L. and F. Norcross, 1861.

Devotions. E.D. to Mary Bowles, August 1861.

Dancing. E.D. to Maria Whitney, 1883; to L. Norcross, December 1861.

Costume. E.D. to L. Norcross, December 1861, with salutation "Dear Peacock." Higginson's remark is from his account of his first interview with E.D., August 16, 1870.

Coward's Choice. E.D. to L. Norcross, December 29, 1861.

The Hunter. E.D. to L. and F. Norcross, 1861.

Verdict Requested. E.D. to T. W. Higginson, April 15, 1862. Higginson's comments are from his *Atlantic Monthly* article of 1891.

Evasion. E.D. to T. W. Higginson, April 25, 1862. William Dean Howells (1837-1920) in his "Editor's Study" in *Harper's New Monthly* magazine, LXXXII, January 1891, observed that the roughness of the poems is deliberate; "It is the soul of an abrupt, exalted New England woman that speaks in such brokenness." Higginson had written that her poems would seem to some as having been "torn up by the roots." Examining the exchange of correspondence between E.D. and Higginson over the years, Conrad Aiken noted that her letters to Higginson "show the wayward pupil replying with a humility, beautiful and pathetic, but remaining singularly, with unmalleable obstinancy, herself." Her "highly individual gift, and the singular sharp beauty, present everywhere, of her personality" he wrote, "suffice to put her among the finest poets in the language."

Song of the Leaf. E.D. to T. W. Higginson, June 8, 1862.

North. E.D. to T. W. Higginson, June 8, 1862.

A Toast. E.D. to T. W. Higginson, April 25, 1862 and July 1862.

Fame. E.D. to T. W. Higginson, June 8, 1862.

The Tested. E.D. to T. W. Higginson (date uncertain).

The Weather in Amherst. E.D. to T. W. Higginson (date uncertain).

The Only Gaze. E.D. to Maria Whitney, 1884; to Mary Bowles, 1862.

The Houseguest. E.D. to L. and F. Norcross, Autumn 1863.

The Covenant. E.D. to L. and F. Norcross, Autumn 1864.

To Target Drawn. E.D. to L. Norcross, February 1865.

The Uninvited. E.D. to Elizabeth Holland, 1865.

The Shipwreck. E.D. to Elizabeth Holland, 1865.

The Wolf. E.D. to Elizabeth Holland, 1866; to Maria Whitney, 1883.
John Cody in a psychoanalytic discussion of oral imagery entitled
"Great Pain" (Cambridge, Mass., 1971) advances the view that
E.D. suffered a total mental collapse just before the onset of her
great creative period, 1858-1862, a breakdown which he thinks
attributable in large part to the inadequacies of Emily Norcross
Dickinson as a mother. Vivian R. Pollak believes, rather, that
Emily's gradual withdrawl from the social world was primarily a
political response to the extreme sex segregation of mid-century
Victorian America, and that "the psychodynamics of the
Dickinson household represented cultural, rather than personal
disease."

Disclosure. E.D. to T. W. Higginson, 1862-63 (?).

A Glee Among the Garrets. The title is derived from Emily Dickinson's
poem which begins "That is solemn we have ended." Rollo May's
words are from his *The Courage to Create.*

A Feast of Absence. E.D. to Elizabeth Holland, 1866.

The Nile. E.D. to Elizabeth Holland, 1866. John Wain comments, "She
broods on death continually, not out of morbidity but because
death is the point at which time-bound human existence abuts
on the timeless. . . . Even in a blankly anti-metaphysical view of
experience, death has the importance that Miss Emily accords to
it, forming as it does the intersection between one dimension
and another."

The Infatuation of Sameness. E.D. to Elizabeth Holland, 1866. Joseph
Lyman lived with the Dickinson family during the winter of
1846 and formed a close platonic attachment to Emily who
appears to have remained his ideal of superior womanhood. The
comment cited above the poem is from a letter to Lyman's
fiancée written in 1858. In 1862 E.D. wrote to Mabel Loomis
Todd, wife of an astronomer at Amherst, and first editor of her
poems and letters: "God's unique capacity is too surprising to
surprise," and in November 1882, to her Norcross cousins, she

138

wrote, "I believe the One who gave us this remarkable earth has the power still further to surprise that which He has caused."
Notes from a Yankee Kitchen. The poem was suggested by Daniel G. Hoffman's comment appearing above it

A Capable Woman. Margaret Maher came from Parish Kilusty in Tipperary. Her letters to a former employer miraculously survived and are preserved in the Burton Historical Collection of the Detroit Public Library; some are owned by Harvard College Library.

PART THREE: AUTUMN SONG

Autumn Song. E.D. to Elizabeth Holland, 1866.

The Key of the Kingdom. E.D. to L. and F. Norcross, 1870 and Spring 1881; also to Holland, 1862.

The Figure in White. As early as 1853, Emily Dickinson had written to a friend, "I do not go from home." She was then 23 years old. By the time she was 30, Conrad Aiken notes, "the habit of sequestration had become distinct." Some commentators feel that it hardened into a mannerism in which she took perverse pleasure. Others see it as a device which freed her to concentrate on her writing.

Recipe. E.D. to L. and F. Norcross, 1870.

The Vicious Visitor. E.D. to L. Norcross, Spring 1871; to L. Norcross, 1860; to Samuel Bowles, 1862.

Father. E.D. to L. and F. Norcross, 1874; to Mary Bowles, January 1878 and April 1880. Edward Norcross died on June 16, 1874, in Boston.

Protection. The incident is fictitious. Conrad Aiken in his introduction to *Selected Poems of Emily Dickinson* (1937), without adequately elaborating it, alludes to an incident in Emily's childhood which might be construed as an example of childhood cruelty to animals, which suggested the poem. The statement by Emily Dickinson was reported by T. W. Higginson in his account of their first interview.

The Word. E.D. to L. Norcross, 1872.

Return of the Dove. E.D. to L. and F. Norcross, Spring 1870.

Cradle Song. Mr. Jay Leyda, in his study of Emily Dickinson, points out that the immigrant Irish had even fewer freedoms than American women. Their religion, he says, made an excellent barrier in the tightly-buttoned Congregationalist villages of Western Massachusetts. He reminds us that even an advanced newspaper like the Springfield Daily *Republican* was "jocular about any local Irish tragedy" while the "civilized" magazine, *Scribner's Monthly*, even as late as the 70's, "supported its shabby Irish anecdotes with threatening editorials." The poverty in which the immigrants lived no doubt contributed to their early death.

Mr. Leyda comments that Emily's interest in birth and death may well have originated or been reinfored by her association with settlement families. Richard and Ann Matthews, English immigrants who worked for the Dickinson family on Pleasant Street, are mentioned in her letters. Ann bore 16 children during Emily's lifetime, nine of whom died. "Although a recluse," Mr. Leyda states, "her circle of friends, acquaintances and correspondents was very large and there appears to have been a continuous exchange with other minds and temperaments. Although ingenious enough to reduce the number of outside pressures to suit the work she was determined to do, there was a point beyond which she could not and would not go in her social housecleaning."

Near and Far. E.D. to L. and F. Norcross, 1873.

Friendship. E.D. to Perez Cowan, 1873.

The Summit. E.D. To F. Norcross, 1873.

Sight. E.D. to L. and F. Norcross, 1873 and 1876.

Strawberries. E.D. to L. and F. Norcross, August 1876.

Love's Fare. E.D. to L. and F. Norcross, 1870.

The Spell. E.D. to L. and F. Norcross, 1873.

The Few. The comment attributed to Emily Dickinson by T. W. Higginson in his account of their first meeting, August 16, 1870.

The Dwelling. E.D. to Abiah Root, January 1851; to L. and F. Norcross, 1873.

The Belle. E.D. to T. W. Higginson, 1879.

Clocks. From Higginson's account of his first meeting with Emily, August 16, 1870.

The Runaway. E.D. to Elizabeth Holland, 1877; to Charles H. Clark, June 16, 1883. The boy's father, Dennis Scannel, worked for the Dickinsons.

Lavinia's Song. E.D. to Maria Whitney, 1884; to T. W. Higginson, 1877.

The Interview. From T. W. Higginson's *Atlantic* essay.

The Fourth of July. E.D. to L. and F. Norcross, July 1879. Emily makes it clear in the letter that Vinnie was trying to calm her sister's fears, whose effort both amused and touched her.

PART FOUR: WINTER SONG

Winter Song. E.D. to L. Norcross, January 1865.

Fragment. E.D. to L. and F. Norcross, 1880; to Mrs. Edward Tuckerman, 1880.

The Guest. E.D. To Mary Bowles, April 1880.

The Empress. E.D. to L. Norcross, Spring 1881.

Tune for a Fiddle. E.D. to L. and F. Norcross, 1881. Henry David Thoreau, 1817-62, was born in Concord, Mass. Conrad Aiken assumes that Emily Dickinson fell prey to the then current Emersonian doctrine of mystical individualism which Henry James noted played almost the part of a social resource in a society lacking entertainment. Aiken also remarks that Emily Dickinson barely mentions in her letters the important literary events which were taking place in her lifetime in America: Emerson lived only 60 miles from her home; Hawthorne was publishing his works during her teens; Poe's works were published in 1850 and Melville brought out *Moby Dick* in 1851; Thoreau's *Walden* appeared when she was 24 and the next year Whitman's *Leaves of Grass.* Other commentators have remarked that the Civil War did not find its way into her work.

Storm. E.D. to James D. Clark, Autumn 1882.

Thanksgiving: 1882. E.D. to O. P. Lord, December 3, 1882.

Harvest. E.D. to Maria Whitney, 1883.

Store. E.D. to Maria Whitney, Summer 1883. See Qur'án 7:172— the question put to "every human being as he comes into existence" is "Am I not your Lord?" to which reply is made "Yea verily, Thou art!"

The Citizen. E.D. to Maria Whitney, 1883.

Mother. E.D. to L. and F. Norcross, November 1882, and to Norcross, 1864. Mrs. Dickinson, who was nursed by Emily during the last 15 years of her life, died in 1882.

Intimations. To Maria Whitney, 1883.

Witchcraft. Louise Bernikow makes the telling point that what is commonly called literary history is actually a record of the choices made by white educated males (in England and America) and reminds us that Emily Dickinson was born at a time and in a culture in which "ladies" were expected to be "charming, acquiescent and voiceless." Dickinson achieved in her poetry something she could not have done by other means without severely dislocating consequences—she "found a voice both original and strange in which to speak the kind of honesty that exists in no other poet of her time, male or female. That voice *is* the poems..." Allen Tate has also commented that Cotton Mather would have had Emily Dickinson "burnt for a witch."

Higginson's Choice. The epigraph is from one of Emily's letters to L. and F. Norcross, 1870.

Conversation. E.D. to Joseph K. Chickering, 1883.

The Seamstress. E.D. to L. Norcross, January 1859—this letter offers evidence that Emily sewed.

The Hearth of Heaven. E.D. to L. and F. Norcross, 1861.

Revenge. E.D. to L. and F. Norcross, July 1884.

Called. E.D. to Abiah Root, January 1851; and to unknown recipient, 1885.

A Pageant of Allegiances. The Irish workers who carried her to the grave she still occupies were Thomas Kelley (leader), Dennis Scannell, Stephen Sullivan, Patrick Ward, Daniel Moynihan and Dennis Cashman. Emily Dickinson died on May 15, 1886.

EPILOGUE

Maggie Saves the Day. The incident of the daguerreotype is mentioned in *Ancestors' Brocades* by Millicent Todd Bingham (Harper and Bros., 1945).

Judge Tenderly. The title alludes, of course, to Emily Dickinson's poem sometimes referred to as her "Letter to the World." It is interesting, in examining her letters and poems, to bear in mind T. S. Eliot's comment that the capacity for writing poetry is rare, as is the capacity for religious emotion, and the appearance of both capacities in one individual rarer still.

BIBLIOGRAPHY

– Principal works cited in epigraphs and notes –

Aiken, Conrad, *Selected Poems of Emily Dickinson*, The Modern Library, New York, 1924.

Bernikow, Louise, "Emily Dickinson," in *The World Split Open*, London, 1974.

Brinnin, John Malcolm, *Emily Dickinson*, ed. Richard Wilbur, The Laurel Poetry Series, New York, 1960.

Hoffman, Daniel G., "Emily Dickinson," in *American Poetry and Poetics*, New York, 1962.

Johnson, Thomas H., *The Letters of Emily Dickinson*, vols. I-III, Cambridge, Mass.: The Belknap Press of Harvard University Press, 1958.

Jones, Peter, "Emily Dickinson," in *An Introduction to Fifty American Poets*, London, 1979.

Leyda, Jay, "Miss Emily's Maggie," in *New World Writing*, No. 3, New York, 1953; *The Years and Hours of Emily Dickinson*, 2 vols., New Haven: Yale University Press, 1960; rpt. Hamden, Conn., Archon Books, 1970.

Linscott, Robert N., *Selected Poems and Letters of Emily Dickinson*, w. Introduction, New York, 1959; selected from *The Complete Poems and Letters of Emily Dickinson*, ed. Thomas H. Johnson, 1955, 1958.

Pollak, Vivian R., *Thirst and Starvation in Emily Dickinson's Poetry*, in *American Literature*, vol. 51, no. 1, March 1979.

Rukeyser, Muriel, "Women of Words," in *The World Split Open*, London, 1974.

Wain, John, "Homage to Emily Dickinson," in *Professing Poetry*, New York, 1977; Middlesex, 1978.

Note: For a comprehensive bibliography, complete through 1968, consult Willis J. Buckingham, ed., *Emily Dickinson: An Annotated Bibliography*. Bloomington and London: Indiana University Press, 1970. Excellent selective bibliographies are found in Jay Leyda's work cited above, and in Richard B. Sewall's *The Life of Emily Dickinson*. New York: Farrar, Straus and Giroux, 1974, 1980. Subscription to *Dickinson Studies* (formerly *Emily Dickinson Bulletin*) and *Higginson Journal* brings contact with a world-wide network of scholars of Dickinson's work and provides outlet for the publication of profiles and studies: address inquiries to Frederick L. Morey, 4508 38th Street, Brentwood, Maryland 20722, U.S.A.